THE COWBOY'S CHALLENGE

CHRISTIAN CONTEMPORARY WESTERN ROMANCE

BRUSH CREEK COWBOYS ROMANCE
BOOK TWO

LIZ ISAACSON

"Watch ye, stand fast in the faith, quit you like men, be strong."

1 Corinthians 16:13

CHAPTER 1

Renee Martin stood on the fringes of the ice cream social, her eyes sweeping the church's multi-purpose room for her cousin. Of course, Leah stood with a group of mostly men, and Renee sighed. Leah would be no help tonight, and Renee straightened her shoulders.

She didn't need help mingling with the townspeople of Brush Creek. She wasn't even sure why she cared; she wasn't a permanent resident of the city. If it could even be called a city. With her, the population barely tipped nine thousand. Of course, Vernal wasn't much bigger. It only seemed that way because of all the tourists going to Dinosaur National Park, where Renee would be starting her new job the following week.

She needed an apartment in Vernal, but she hadn't been able to find one. Truth be told, she hadn't even looked. She pushed away the adult things she didn't want to deal with and focused on the long tables set up along one wall of the room. A bona fide ice cream bar. At least the pastor in Brush Creek knew how to bring people into the church.

A twinge of guilt cut through Renee, but she stuck that back down into her gut too. She liked ice cream. As she smoothed her palms over her shirt and felt the extra layers and curves she had, she knew it was pretty obvious to everyone that she liked a lot of ice cream.

Leah intercepted her before she could join the end of the line. "Come meet these guys." She glanced back over her shoulder to where the pod of males waited.

"Not interested," Renee said without letting her gaze linger on the men. If she did, she'd surely find one she found attractive, only to have Leah choose him as her next boyfriend. It had happened before, twice.

Leah laughed like Renee had just said the wittiest thing on the planet. Renee rolled her eyes and tossed her dark brown hair over her shoulder. "Leah, stop it. Have you already forgotten the disaster you created for me only two days ago?"

Leah sobered and blinked as if she had truly forgotten. "What? That thing with Justin Jackman?" She waved her hand like she was swatting away an annoying fly. "That was nothing. He's too uptight anyway."

Renee reached for a plastic bowl and handed it to Leah before taking one for herself. She'd thought Justin was cute, but she hadn't been properly informed of the situation before going in. She wouldn't make that mistake again.

"You should've mentioned that you'd dated him." She picked up a spoon and a napkin.

Leah scoffed. "It was barely four or five dates. I didn't think it mattered."

"Obviously, it did." Renee scooped several slices of banana into the bottom of her bowl. If there was anything better than a mint chocolate chip banana split, Renee didn't want to know about it. Her hips were already two sizes too big. "And I didn't think Justin was uptight."

That caught Leah's attention, and Renee's stomach twisted. Why hadn't she learned to keep her big mouth shut around Leah?

"Really? You liked Justin?" For some reason, her cousin thought it was her life's mission to find Renee a boyfriend. If Renee had been any good at doing so herself, she might have resisted harder. At least she'd had a few years at college without Leah's constant meddling—and Renee had dated exactly one man. The relationship hadn't gone anywhere, and they still kept up with each other online and through texts.

"I didn't *like* him," she said. "I just thought—"

"Renee, hello." The pastor stood in front of the ice cream tubs, beaming at her. "It's good to see you."

Renee smiled and said, "Hello, Pastor Peters. I'll have the mint chocolate chip."

He dug his scoop into the appointed tub and gave her two perfectly sculpted spheres of ice cream. Her mouth watered and she wondered if she could escape Leah so she could enjoy her treat instead of standing with a group of men, nibbling around the edge of the sundae while she pretended to dislike ice cream.

She'd just spooned hot fudge into her dish when Leah said, "Well, here's your second chance, Ren. Justin just walked in."

"Leah, don't you dare. I just want to eat my ice cream,

chat with a few ladies from the knitting club, and go home."

Leah laughed again, and Renee swore she added extra decibels just to get people to look. Thankfully, Justin wasn't one of them. But a couple of Leah's girlfriends must've known the laugh was the Bat Signal, because they swarmed.

"Hey, girls," Tawny, a tall leggy blonde, said. "Have you tried the mocha caramel crunch?" She took a bite and moaned. "It is to die for."

"Who looks interesting tonight?" Karla asked, glancing around. She carried a bowl of mostly melted ice cream, and her narrow waist testified of her self-control over the best treat on the planet. "There's a few guys here from Beaverton that look like they might be fun."

Renee tried to edge away, but Leah said, "Ladies, tonight is all about Renee," and her feet grew roots. She even forgot about her banana split though she still held the bowl.

Tawny squealed and turned in a full circle. "Who's the lucky guy?"

Renee's stomach fell all the way to the floor. "Leah, no."

"Justin Jackman." Leah slid her spoon into her mouth with a satisfied smile. "I dare you to go over there and ask him out."

"I am not doing that," Renee hissed. "I already made a fool of myself in front of him. He clearly wasn't interested."

"You didn't even try the other night."

"I did," Renee said, and she'd detailed everything she'd said to Justin. He wasn't uptight, like Leah claimed. He simply wasn't interested in Renee. He'd made that much clear, and though it had stung, Renee wasn't that broken up about it. Sure, he had thick, brown hair and blazing blue eyes that seemed to see more than just Renee's physical features. She'd liked that, but with only one real relationship under her belt, she was rusty on her small talk skills.

"It's a bet," Leah said, digging in her pocket and pulling out a twenty. "What have you girls got?"

Renee felt the ground slipping from beneath her feet. "Guys, no," she tried anyway. But in only seconds, the pile of cash in Leah's hand had reached a hundred dollars. She stared it, her mouth salivating in the same way it had over the mint chocolate chip ice cream. She'd graduated two weeks ago, jobless, with nowhere to go and nothing to do. She'd never wanted a career. Growing up, all Renee had ever wanted to do was get married and have children.

But she'd need more than a few dates for that to happen. So she'd moved in with Leah and done one adult thing: applied for jobs at the nearby National Parks. Utah had a lot of them, and Dinosaur had bitten. Thankfully, it was only a forty-five minute drive from Brush Creek.

Renee knew it was time to grow up and start taking care of things; become self-reliant. But just because she was twenty-four and a college graduate didn't mean she knew what to do with her life.

"One hundred fifteen dollars and twenty-one cents," Leah declared, and Renee's resolve died. She needed the money.

"Fine." She handed her bowl to Karla and ran her fingers through her hair. "What do I have to do?"

"Get a date with the hunky cowboy, and this is all yours." She flapped the bills in Renee's face. She made a swipe for it, though her cousin ran a couple of miles every day and could certainly take Renee before she reached the exit.

Renee straightened her blouse and fluffed her hair again. She located Justin standing with another cowboy who had a blonde-haired woman on his arm and two boys in front of them in line.

She could just pretend she hadn't gotten any ice cream yet. Adding confidence to her step, she strode toward the ice cream bar again. Justin didn't glance at her or turn toward her when she sidled up behind him.

Standing there, extreme awkwardness descended on her. Just when she was about to reach out and tap his shoulder, he twisted slightly toward her and retrieved something from his pocket. He glanced in her direction as a capsule of orange Tic Tacs made an appearance.

Her dang saliva glands were really having a workout. She'd grown up eating orange Tic Tacs like they were candy, not breath fresheners.

"Hey," she said as he threw back a palmful of the orange mints.

A sour look crossed his face, but it could've been from the overload of Tic Tacs. "Hey." He turned back to his friends, but he was clearly a fifth wheel with the family in front of him, and Renee seized onto that fact.

"What's your favorite ice cream?" she asked as she picked up a second bowl.

"I'm a purist," he said. "Vanilla bean." He bypassed the bananas too.

Renee didn't understand him at all, despite the orange Tic Tac connection. "No toppings?"

"I like caramel, chocolate, and pecans."

"Oh, pecans. Fancy." She trilled out a giggle, hoping to draw him into a real conversation once they made it through the line.

He stared at her for a moment past comfortable and inched down the line—toward the pastor.

Renee's heart seized, then started beating at triple-time. Her first impulse was to duck out of line, and fast. Only sheer desire for the money kept her in place at Justin's side. And the vanilla tub sat way down on the end of the ice cream bar.

"They've set tables up out on the lawn," she said. "Were you going to go out there?"

"I hadn't really thought about it." Justin looked at her and flashed her a smile. "Is there shade?"

She grinned full-force at him. "I saw some umbrellas on the way in."

He glanced over his shoulder to his friends, but they'd already gotten their ice cream and were sprinkling nuts and candies on them. They didn't seem to notice that he'd fallen behind. He turned back to her and scanned her from her wedge-sandaled feet to the top of her head. His features softened as he drank in her kinky-curled hair.

"Probably better than hanging out with my boss."

"Hello, Justin," Pastor Peters said. "Good to see you down here this evening."

"First day of good weather," Justin said. "My boss insisted we get off the ranch."

"How are things with the horses?"

"Good." Justin exhaled and a strange look passed through his eyes. "Good."

Pastor Peters focused on hers, his eyes pleasant if not a bit surprised. "Renee. Coming back for seconds?"

All her muscles seized. She couldn't seem to look away from Justin, who settled all his weight on his left foot, away from her, and waited for her explanation.

She couldn't say that she hadn't eaten her original bowl. Or that she'd come over here on a bet, simply because Justin was at the end of the line.

"I only had one bite," she finally managed to say. "My cousin—" Justin visibly flinched, but Renee plowed on. "I gave her my bowl for a friend."

Pastor Peters didn't seem to have a problem with her rather lame explanation. He nodded and asked, "Mint chocolate chip again?"

"Yes, please." Relief tumbled through her when Justin's lip curled upward and he moved on to the hot fudge. Renee pressed her eyes closed and wondered how long it would take before she blurted out that she'd split the money with him if he'd just say he asked her out.

Chapter 2

Justin had no idea if Renee Martin was telling the truth or not. He liked the way her hair sprouted from her scalp like snakes, wondered what it would feel like between his fingers. It only reached her chin, and he liked the curly bob a lot. He liked her green-hazel eyes, the color of the pond water out on the ranch, and her pale-as-cream skin dotted with the prettiest freckles he ever did see. She seemed exactly like the type of woman he would normally date.

But she was also Leah's cousin, and Justin didn't want anything to do with her. She'd set him up before, with a woman named Paulette, and that relationship had taken Justin all the way to the altar. If Paulette had shown up, he'd be married today.

But she hadn't. And the whole blasted town knew it. Justin hadn't dated seriously since. Even his stint with Leah he didn't consider true dating. She probably knew it too. That was why he'd avoided her whenever he came down to town.

But Renee was new in Brush Creek...she didn't know about the near-wedding-turned-disaster that had happened two summers ago. Justin tamped down the idea to ask Renee to go with him to the rodeo. Landon Edmunds, the owner of the ranch where Justin worked, had assigned Justin to go to the rodeo in Vernal and meet with the PRCA reps. He also had appointments with three bronc riders and four barrel racers who wanted to know more about Brush Creek Horse Ranch and what kind of horses they trained.

And Paulette would be there, sporting her biggest hairstyle and most glittery cowgirl hat as she rode Daisy May—the horse Justin had trained especially for her. He wouldn't mind seeing the horse, but the woman....

Justin just needed a date. Then Paulette wouldn't get under his skin. He cut a glance at Renee, wondering if she was really interested in him or not. He appreciated the curve of her hips and the way she didn't take dainty bites of ice cream.

He swallowed and sat on a bench in the shade, Renee right next to him. "It's not too bad in the shade," he said, cursing himself for talking about the weather. He hadn't been out of the dating game that long, had he?

"It's still early in June." She scooped up a bite of banana, mint ice cream, and hot fudge. The flavor combination sounded gross to Justin, but she seemed to like it.

She put her spoon in her half-empty bowl. "Okay, look. My friends dared me to come talk to you tonight." She looked at him with apprehension in her eyes. "There was money involved, so one might consider it a bet." She tried on a smile, but it came across her full lips fast and left quickly.

The ice cream in Justin's stomach sent waves of coldness through him. "Oh." He blinked and took another bite, focusing on the horizon instead of Renee's pretty face. "So you're not really interested in me."

"No, I am," she said. "You're the one who blew me off the other night."

He appraised her, trying to figure out what had happened a couple of nights ago at the country line dance and what was happening now. "What do you have to do to win the bet?"

"Get a date with you. I'll give you half of the money. We can eat a hot dog from the cart at the park. Ten minutes, tops."

Justin tipped his head back and laughed. "Renee, you're worth more than ten minutes and a hot dog from a cart."

She lifted her eyes to his, confusion racing through her intoxicating gaze. "Thank you?"

"You don't have to say it like it's a question." Justin scooped another bite of ice cream into his mouth. "I will say I've never been picked up in a bar before."

"This isn't a bar."

"I believe the flyer said ice cream bar right on it." He flashed her a flirty look. "And on a bet too."

"So...are you asking me out?"

He noted that Walker and Tess hadn't come to find him. He hadn't wanted to leave the ranch tonight, but Walker had insisted everyone take the night off and Justin didn't have anything else to do. With his truck broken down, it was either this ice cream bar at the church, or a movie he'd already seen with Ted.

"Have you ever been to the rodeo?"

"I went to college in Denver," she said.

"I don't see how that answers my question."

"Lots of rodeos in the Denver area. So yes, I've been to a few rodeos."

"I need to go to one next weekend, and I'd love to have someone to go with."

She set her empty bowl on the bench next to her and scooted an inch closer to him. His heart leapt and he looked at her hands in her lap. Slender fingers, with pale-pink painted nails.

"This sounds like a non-date," she said.

"I have to go for work," he said. "And since you told me about the bet, I'll say that I normally don't take a date when it's for work, but...." His words stuck in his throat.

"Another woman," Renee said. "You need me to look pretty on your arm so she'll be jealous."

Justin didn't like the way that sounded. "That's almost right," he said. "But I don't care if she's jealous. I just don't want her to think I haven't moved on."

"So she was a serious girlfriend."

"Yes," Justin choked out. He hadn't finished his ice cream, but it sounded unappetizing after this conversation so he set the bowl on the ground. He didn't need to bring up the word *fiancé* right now.

"I'd love to go to the rodeo with you." She slipped her arm into his elbow, and the gesture reminded him of how old he was. He wondered how old Renee was—she was clearly much younger than him. The way she dressed, and spoke, and acted testified of it. Her relation to Leah wasn't the only reason he'd walked away from her at the diner the other night.

He'd actually found her giggling annoying. Her hair fluffing juvenile. Her inability to leave her gaggle of girlfriends to have a real conversation infuriating. So he'd left her, disinterested in being her latest boy toy.

But now, sitting with her in the shade, she didn't seem to be the same woman at all.

"How old are you?" he asked.

She tilted her head back and met his eyes. "Twenty-four. You."

He gulped and pushed his cowboy hat forward with his free hand. "A lot older than that."

A hint of a smile touched her lips. "How much older?"

"Eight years older," he said. Almost a decade.

"Ever been married?"

"There you are." Graham, Tess's son, came skidding up to him. "We're leavin'. You ready to go?"

He stood, glad for the interruption. "Give me two minutes, okay?" Graham ran off, and Justin saw Walker waiting on the sidewalk. Though his cowboy hat obscured his face, Justin knew he was watching.

He turned back to Renee, who had also risen to her feet. "Maybe you'll give me your phone number, and I can call you." He gazed at her evenly, his heart bobbing against his voice box.

She giggled, and he imagined he might have to get used to the sound if he wanted to be with her. "Of course you can."

He held out his phone and she plucked it from his

fingers. She tapped and swiped and handed the device back. "There you go. I'm a night owl." She turned and pranced across the lawn, turning back to give him a finger wave when she reached the doorway. Then she disappeared inside.

Justin sighed and faced his friends, sure Tess would question him relentlessly on the way back to the ranch. It was only fifteen minutes; surely Justin could weather that. He crossed the lawn to the sidewalk, and no sooner had his boot hit cement did Tess ask, "Who was that? She's pretty."

Justin ducked his head. "Her name's Renee Martin."

"Isn't that—?"

"No," Justin said loudly over Walker's question. He'd mentioned Renee to Walker while they worked in the horse arena the day after the dance. He knew the words he'd used, and he didn't want to hear them. *Annoying brunette.*

"She's too young for me," he said as he got in the truck. "So it's not a big deal."

"But you got her number," Tess persisted.

"How do you know?"

"I saw you give her your phone."

Justin glared at her. "We're going to the rodeo together, all right?"

"Because of Paulette?" Walker asked. "I told you I'd go to the rodeo."

Justin shook his head. "Tess has to go to Evanston that same weekend. It's fine. I'm going with Renee. I can handle Paulette." Justin spoke with confidence, but he didn't feel it inside. He was over Paulette; he didn't want her back in his life. But he didn't want her to know that he didn't have anyone in his life.

Several minutes passed, and Justin thought maybe he'd escape the questions tonight. Then Tess said, "How old is she?" and Justin pressed his eyes closed and prayed for patience.

———

THE NEXT MORNING, before the sun had fully risen, Justin clucked at the horse, a pretty little mare that shone red in the approaching sunlight. She eyed him with a wildness he'd coach out of her over the course of the next six months. He'd named her Red Star, and he had an inkling she'd win a team roping event or two. Or twenty. She had the powerful legs to be a heeler, if she'd just trust Justin.

She dodged right, and Justin let her go. She paced, and he kept the pole tapping on the ground, kept her moving. Red Star finally settled into the circle, though she kept up the trot for several more minutes.

"Walk," he commanded her, and her step slowed. Her head lowered. The crazed look in her eye had died as she expended her energy. He retracted the pole to urge her closer to the center. The bag rustled along the dirt and Red Star snorted.

After another half hour of waiting for her to give in, she finally nosed him, her feet straddling the pole she seemed to hate so much. Justin gave her the affection she'd earned. He just wished she'd get there a little faster. She hadn't been making progress in about a week, and it still took her about an hour to come to him. Until she'd trust him right out of the gate, he couldn't train her to be a rodeo champion.

He brushed her down and fed her an extra slice of hay

from a nearby bale. "There you go. No oats today. Gotta come in faster." She hung her head over the stall door like she really felt bad. He chuckled and stroked her nose before heading back to the barn. Walker would have more for him to do, as the chores around the ranch seemed never-ending.

But Justin wouldn't have his life any other way. He adored working outside in the fresh air. He loved everything about horses. He'd competed in the pro rodeo circuit for eight years, winning every year in team roping, before retiring to Brush Creek. He wasn't in the rodeo, but he was near enough not to miss it.

In the barn, Walker stood over a table with Landon Edmunds. Walker was the foreman, which meant he made sure the four other cowboys who lived on-site showed up and did the jobs he assigned to them. Landon owned the ranch, which meant he financed everything and held the vision he wanted for Brush Creek Horse Ranch. He'd started it six years ago, with two horses and a dream. The ranch now produced about a dozen horses for the rodeo circuit every year, and they each brought a pretty penny to the trainer who worked with them.

Landon only employed former rodeo stars, and Justin felt lucky to have gotten on at Brush Creek immediately after he'd decided to leave the circuit.

"What's goin' on?" he asked as both Walker and Landon looked concerned. Justin glanced at the table, where a blueprint sat. "What is that?"

"New watering system," Landon said. "For the hay fields behind the cabins." He leaned away from the table and then took several steps away, one hand rubbing up and down the back of his head.

"It's expensive," Walker said by way of explanation. "But it would cut down on the hours we spend out in the fields."

"By fifty percent," Landon said. "And with that much extra time, we could train two more horses a year. And that would pay for the system in just two years."

"Sounds like it's worth it." Justin thumped the table with a fist. "What's next for me?"

"The disc mower is on the fritz again, and I need you to work your magic on it." Walker reached for a folder on the back corner of the table. "And then you have a customer coming at three."

"A customer?" The two horses he was currently training wouldn't be ready for months, and Walker didn't usually have his men train three horses at a time.

"Yeah, an Abby Guzman. She wants to know about horseback riding lessons for her son. Guess his dad was a header, and the boy's interested in it as well."

Justin made a face. "I don't do horseback riding lessons."

"She'd eventually need a proper header horse," Walker said, snapping the folder closed and handing it to him. "And you're our team roping expert, so I gave her to you."

Justin flipped open the folder but didn't really read anything. "Does she live in Brush Creek?"

"Vernal, but she's comin' up here. Three o'clock." Walker started to walk away with Landon, and Justin looked at the folder. He scanned until he found how old the boy was. Five.

Justin's stomach fell. He definitely didn't want to do

horseback riding lessons with a five-year-old. He'd just have to find a way to get rid of Abby Guzman.

CHAPTER 3

Justin: What's your favorite color?

Renee: Pink. Or maybe yellow. Something bright. You?

Justin: Blue.

Renee: You seem like a blue person. You were wearing a blue shirt at the ice cream social.

Justin: That was a bar. Did you get your money for winning the bet?

Renee: Yes, all $115, so we can eat out somewhere nice before the rodeo!

Justin: It's not for two more weeks. Not sure if I told you that.

Renee: You did. I have it on my calendar.

Justin: Great. And we might have to make dinner into lunch. I have a lot to do there, and it's not usually during the actual rodeo.

Renee: Whatever you need.

Justin: All right, well, it's late, and I have to work early. Talk to you tomorrow.

———

RENEE: Haven't heard from you today. You alive?

Justin, seventeen minutes later: Yeah, but barely. Rough day of training today, and I started horseback riding lessons with a kid.

Renee: A kid, huh? How old?

Justin: Five.

Renee: Can anyone take horseback riding lessons out at the ranch?

Justin: Trust me, you don't want to take horseback riding lessons.

Renee: Why not?

Justin: Just come on out, and I'll take you for a ride.

Renee: Is that what you do for fun? Ride your horse around in the wilderness?

Justin: Sometimes. I like to hike, fish, and ride four-wheelers too.

Renee: I like to read.

Justin: I literally can't think of the last book I read.

Renee: I read four last week. Oh! And I'm starting my new job on Monday.

Justin: What will you be doing?

Renee: Working for the National Parks Department at Dinosaur National Monument.

Justin: Fancy.

Renee: I'll be handing out maps and taking park admissions. LOL. It won't be anything to write home about.

Justin: Do you do that a lot? Write home, I mean.

Renee: Sometimes.

Justin: Tell me about your family.

———

RENEE COULDN'T TYPE that much, so she pressed the call button and waited while Justin's phone rang.

"Hi," he said easily, his voice soft and full of a smile.

"Hi." Her adrenaline rushed through her "I thought it might be easier to just call about the family thing."

"Oh yeah? Lots to say, huh?"

She laughed, her curls touching her shoulders as she leaned her head back. "I guess so. My family is really large."

"Define 'large'."

"I have nine siblings."

Justin sucked in a breath. "Wow, that is large."

She giggled. "What was your definition of large?"

"I have two brothers," he said. "They're both married and have a few kids each. It feels like a lot of people when we get together."

"How often do you get together?"

"I'm from Kentucky," he said. "I only see them a couple of times a year."

Renee cocked her head to the side, listening for something in the empty spaces. "How long has it been since you've been home?"

"I like the texting version of Twenty Questions better." A soft rumble of laughter came through the line, tickling her eardrums and accelerating her pulse.

"Oh, come on. I could just tell you weren't telling the truth." Renee glanced at the door as a noise sounded beyond it. Leah had probably just gotten home from her evening run.

"You could? How?"

"I don't know. It's just like a sixth sense I have." She pulled the phone from her mouth as Leah knocked on the door. Renee opened it and gestured with the phone. Leah raised her hand and backed away, a knowing smile in her eyes. At least she wouldn't demand Renee give the money back.

"I haven't been home in a couple of years," he said. "But I have usually gone home for at least Thanksgiving or Christmas. Sometimes in the summer, if my boss makes me."

"Why would he make you?"

"Because." He exhaled heavily, and she could picture him kicked back with his boots off, his cowboy hat tilted slightly on his head. "The work on a ranch is never over. So I don't really ever take or get days off."

"I had no idea."

"Tell me about your new job."

Renee had noted that Justin didn't give many details about himself but continually asked for hers. She didn't mind. She laid back on the bed and started detailing the first real job she'd ever had—and she hadn't even started yet.

Renee really hoped she didn't hate it. Standing in a booth on the side of the road didn't sound terribly exciting, but anything was better than refilling salad bar containers or getting up at three a.m. to clean the student center on campus.

Justin yawned, and Renee realized she'd been talking for a while now. "I'm so sorry," she said. "It's almost ten o'clock."

That sexy chuckle came through the line again, and he

said, "I like listenin' to your pretty voice. Call me tomorrow?"

Warmth wove through her. She smiled. "Sure. Tomorrow." She ended the call and stayed still, at least on the outside. On the inside, she quaked with nerves, with emotions she hadn't felt in the longest time.

She was excited about something for the first time in years. A new job. A possible new boyfriend.... Her heart thu-thumped and she propelled herself off the bed, a smile so large her cheeks hurt on her face. She found Leah in the living room, half-asleep in front of the television.

She sighed the kind of sigh that said, *I'm so happy*, and Leah glanced at her. "Look at you. Talking to *Justin*?"

"Yeah."

"He talk much?"

Renee's good mood deflated slightly. "He talked a normal amount." She closed her eyes and leaned her head back against the couch, a prayer of gratitude in her heart that she'd come to Brush Creek, even if her stay here was only temporary.

Maybe it doesn't have to be, she thought. But by the time she made the nearly-hour-long drive to work on Monday, she knew she couldn't live in Brush Creek and work at Dinosaur. She needed a place in Vernal, then the drive would only be fifteen minutes. But then she'd have to drive to see Justin.

She pulled into the appointed staff lot and pulled out her phone. *Made it to work! Hope you have a great day.* She sent the text to Justin and climbed from her car, ready to face whatever this day held. It was the first day of her adult life, after all, and she wanted to be brave about it.

CHAPTER 4

Justin didn't see Renee in the flesh for several days. The horseback riding lessons had quickly become his most dreaded task on the ranch, because they took up his free time in the evenings. The disc mower seemed to have a personal vendetta against him, and it kept breaking down. The prep for planting had slowed to almost a crawl, and Justin wasn't the only cowboy at Brush Creek Ranch that was pulling double shifts.

He spoke to Renee every night when she called, and they had lengthy text conversations. Justin liked this new, technological style of dating. He could be available even when he wasn't available. He could take his time to answer questions instead of getting put on the spot, and he could even choose to ignore something he didn't want to talk about.

Renee didn't seem to have anything she didn't want to talk about. Justin entered the barn the night before the rodeo to silence, and he was glad for it. His English shepherd trotted ahead of him, heading straight for the tack room where the treats were. Justin stopped by and grabbed one of the rawhide chews and gave it to Roy, who settled down with the bone between his paws. He'd be good for a while, and Justin gave the dog an affectionate pat on his way to the stables in the back of the barn.

He'd been using a tall bay horse the color of fresh churned butter for the riding lessons. "Hey, Magic." He unlatched the gate and stepped into the stall with the horse. He ran his hand along his nose and down the horse's neck and back. "You ready for Carson again tonight?"

The horse didn't twitch a muscle, a testament to his training. Landon really was a genius with horses, a real-live horse whisperer. Justin saddled Magic and led him out to the outdoor arena. The evening heat hung in the air, shimmering on the horizon. Justin let himself enjoy the view, the red-and-white striped rocks in the butte beyond the ranch, the scent of sage in the air, the sky bleeding all the colors of an old bruise.

The sound of tires on gravel alerted him to Abby and Carson's arrival, and Justin stuck a smile on his face. Abby had long hair the color of ripe wheat, and her son did too. The little boy bounded toward Justin and the riding ring while Abby hung back by the car. She'd eventually approach the railing and watch as Justin gave Carson commands.

Tonight that happened about halfway through. Justin kept an eye on her, the horse and boy, and his watch. Finally, the lesson ended, and Carson ran happily off with Justin's dog. Abby dug in her pocket for a twenty-dollar bill, but she hesitated before handing it to him.

She tilted her head, the ranch lamps and her turquoise

eyes sparkling. "Hey, would you want to get dinner some time after lessons?"

Justin froze. His mouth turned dry, his muscles sagged. He breathed and he blinked, both involuntary reactions. Abby was closer to his age; only a year younger than him. She was pretty, and she clearly adored her son. Justin had no idea what she did for a living, or where her husband was, or how he could make a relationship work with her in Vernal.

Plus, he was already...what? What was he doing with Renee? Texting and phone calls wasn't dating. He'd seen her twice in the last couple of weeks, and the first time he'd never wanted to cross paths with her again.

Abby's dazzle dulled, and she fell back a step. "It's okay, Justin."

"I'm seeing someone already," he blurted out, though his brain reeled that maybe Abby was a better match for him. She didn't giggle, and she didn't tell long stories, and she appeared to have her life somewhat put together.

"I see," Abby said, turning now and striding away from him. She twisted back. "Oh, the money." She stepped back over to him and handed him the twenty with a smile so fast he barely saw it. "Thank you. See you next week."

He stared at the money in his palm, everything in his mind spinning. He finally called out, "I'm sorry, Abby," but she didn't turn or otherwise acknowledge that he'd spoken. He turned around, frustrated, and found Magic staring at him placidly. "That was awkward, wasn't it?" He reached for the horse's reins.

"Sure was." Walker emerged from the shadows and slapped together a pair of work gloves. Dust flung into the air and hung in the light.

Justin gave him a glare but said nothing. He set out for the barn, hoping Walker would finish whatever he was doing and leave him alone. He followed Justin into the barn, where Ted, one of the best bronc riders the rodeo had ever seen, stood with Landon.

A groan escaped Justin's mouth. This was going to be a real show. He loved the men he worked with. Ted and Walker were his neighbors, one on each side of his cabin. They all had dogs, like Justin did, and Ted usually strummed a guitar in the evenings on his back porch. Justin kept his windows open anytime the weather was halfway decent so he could hear it.

When Paulette had stood him up on their wedding day, it had been Walker who'd finally pulled Justin from the altar. Ted who'd driven him back to Brush Creek, and Landon who'd given his life purpose. They hadn't judged him or treated him like he was broken, though he couldn't remember much that had happened in the couple of months that had followed the incident.

Ted and Landon talked, glancing at Justin as he plodded by with the horse. He acknowledged them but kept going. Walker thankfully veered into the tack room, and a small measure of relief spiraled through Justin. His phone buzzed in his back pocket, but he ignored it. He knew it would be Renee, and he didn't want to talk right now.

His brain buzzed like a hive of bees. He hadn't felt so out of control since Paulette's departure. He didn't like the feeling of being on a roller coaster. Up one moment. Down the next. Wrench around that emotional curve. He'd grown accustomed to the stability in his life, in finding peace in the simple act of brushing down a horse and putting him away for the night.

As Justin crossed the lane from the ranch to his cabin, he finally landed on the center of his concerns: Renee. He sure liked having someone who didn't work on the ranch to talk to. At the same time, the woman worked an hour away, and surely she wouldn't be staying in Brush Creek permanently. She hadn't said so in those exact words, but she had implied her living situation with her cousin was temporary.

Justin set the coffee maker, a deep weariness for this day in his bones. He tossed his phone on the kitchen counter and washed his hands while he watched the blinking green light indicating he'd missed a call.

Ideas revolved in his head, but he couldn't seem to grasp onto one and think about it for any length of time. Coffee started to drip and the smell filled the house and calmed him. His mother always made coffee, any time of day or night, when they'd had a problem to solve. With a mug of the steaming liquid in his hands, he headed for his bedroom. One sip, and his tense muscles released. Two sips, and a plan formed.

He'd shower, and then he'd call Renee. He wasn't really "seeing her," as he'd told Abby. But they had started something, and he needed to get some things straight before he did see her in the flesh tomorrow.

———

JUSTIN'S PULSE stormed through his veins as he drove down the canyon to the town. Renee lived with Leah on the north side of town, about as far from Vernal as one could get. She had confirmed in real words last night that she wouldn't be living with Leah for much longer. How much longer, she hadn't been able to say.

He'd been up for hours following the conversation, the combination of news he didn't want to hear and four cups of coffee making sleep nearly impossible. He yawned as he pulled into a driveway he'd parked in before. Renee spilled from the house wearing a white sundress covered with large splotches of blue flowers.

She looked amazing with her hair tumbling from her head in those crazy curls. A smile lit her face when Justin slid from the truck, and he reached for her hand as if it were the most natural thing in the world. So maybe he'd thought her immature and annoying the first time they'd met. Maybe she did talk too much. But seeing her, touching her, holding her hand in his, Justin was reminded of all the things he liked about her.

"Hey." He pulled her to him and took a deep breath of her hair. He stood taller than her. So tall, she could lay her cheek against his collarbone in an embrace. She smiled up at him and brushed an errant curl from her face with her free hand.

"Hey, yourself." She stepped back. "Is this okay for the rodeo?"

He scanned her again, curves and all. "You said you've been to a rodeo before." He walked her around the front of his truck and opened the passenger door.

"I have."

"Then you should know there's more dirt than people." He drank in the dress again. "And that dress is white." He grinned as she looked down at her clothes as if she couldn't remember what she'd picked.

"I'm not going to be riding a horse or anything." She looked up at him with a hint of fear in her eyes. "Right?"

He squeezed her hand. "You never know."

Pure panic raced across her face. "Justin."

He laughed and nudged her toward getting in the truck. "I was kidding. I'm sure it'll be fine." He didn't mention the dirty, dusty bleachers they'd have to sit on to watch the rodeo. If the woman wanted to wear a white dress to the rodeo, he wasn't going to stop her.

With her settled, Justin went around and got behind the wheel. He reached for his package of Tic Tacs and downed as many as would come out of the container. He offered it to Renee, who shook her head with a small smile.

"What?" he asked.

"You eat those like candy."

"I like them. They're certainly not mints."

"I used to do that when I was a kid."

He shrugged. "I carry them all the time. Our new horses don't like the sound, and it's my job to get them to become perfectly compliant."

"Do you like other flavors, or only orange?"

"I figure if I have to carry this container around all the time, I might as well get some benefit out of it. I only like the orange ones. Landon buys them in bulk for me."

She slid across the bench seat and sat right next to him. His heart tripped as he accelerated on the highway leading out of town and into Vernal. "What do the other boys like?"

Justin sighed, his grip on the steering wheel tightening.

"Let's see. Landon likes the white ones. Walker too. Ted and Grant will take whatever, even this new grape-lime flavor." He shuddered. "They're disgusting."

She giggled, and somehow the sound didn't worm its way under Justin's skin and aggravate him. He reached for her hand, glad when she gave it to him. Her fingers felt cool and smooth between his, and his nerves settled further.

By the time they arrived at the restaurant she'd chosen for lunch, Justin wasn't sure why he'd been so worked up about possibly dating Renee. Their conversations had always been easy. He'd thought it was because of the distance between them while they talked, but it had been just as comfortable in the truck. He held the door for her to go first into the restaurant, and the flirtatious look she gave him as she passed solidified what he'd been wondering about.

They were definitely seeing each other. A smile formed on his face, and he only managed to wipe it away a moment before Renee turned to look at him.

His enjoyment and peace only lasted until they pulled into the rodeo grounds. "Most of this will be boring," he said, reaching to the seat behind him to grab a briefcase bag. It held a dozen folders, his schedule for the afternoon, and their rodeo tickets for that evening.

"You're welcome to come with me, but I need a favor." He withdrew the first folder and extended it toward her. "Will you pretend to be my assistant? These are—" He swallowed. "Business meetings, and I...."

Renee looked at the folder and then him. "You what?"

Justin looked at her evenly, trying not to fall into her

gorgeous hazel eyes. "I don't quite know how to introduce you."

A blush stained her cheeks, making her even more beautiful, and she took the folder. "I can be your assistant, sure."

"The date part—I mean, we just went to lunch. That was a date, right? And now we have to work, and then we'll go to the rodeo. It's like work sandwiched by a date."

She grinned. "Does it count as two dates, do you think?"

He had no idea why it mattered. "Sure, if you want it to."

"Oh, I do." Her expression went from flirty to sexy, and Justin needed to get out of the truck before he did something he couldn't explain.

He practically jumped from the cab and took a long drag of fresh air. The oxygen helped infuse some reason into his brain, but the attraction between him and Renee lingered long after he'd finally cleared his head.

CHAPTER 5

Renee smiled and flounced from appointment to appointment, flipping open folders and shaking hands with the bronc riders and barrel racers as she played the part of Justin's perfect assistant. No one seemed to think she wasn't, and no one asked her any questions. Thankfully.

She got distracted by Justin's beautiful bass voice several times. He could make Appaloosas and pinto horses sound sexier than she thought possible. She schooled her thoughts, sure it was time to stop acting like a teenager and start acting like a college graduate. An adult.

The blonde who seemed to have more hair than humanly possible finally left them alone again.

"All done," Justin said.

Renee sighed with relief. "Wow, that was a lot of appointments."

He flipped a page in a folder he'd pulled out himself and had never relinquished to her. He scratched something out and then closed the folder, a heavy sigh escaping his mouth too. He met her eyes and gave her a lazy grin that heated her blood past comfortable.

"Yeah, but I got four new horse deals today." He stood and gave her the folder to put back in the briefcase bag. "And I'm starving. Let's walk over to the carnival and get a funnel cake. You want to?"

She slipped the folder into the bag. "Fried dough with sugar and cream? I'm in." Renee noticed the way his eyes skated down the length of her body, and supreme satisfaction sang through her.

Justin shouldered the bag and threaded his fingers through hers. "You can get all kinds of fried things at the carnival. My favorite are the foot-long corndogs."

Renee's mouth watered at the same time her stomach revolted. "That is too much food."

"Oh, please," he said, his voice flirtatious. "You ate two bowls of ice cream at the church social."

She laughed, the pleasure of being here with Justin almost too much. Though she carried a fair few pounds more than normal, her steps felt light as air as they left the rodeo grounds and crossed the street to the carnival.

It was still early, and the crowds of teenagers that would descend at night were still a couple of hours away. Families had likely come this morning right after the parade she'd read about online. At four-thirty, the carnival grounds were mostly deserted, leaving the path to the food alley clear.

Justin ordered two funnel cakes, one with powdered sugar and one with strawberries and cream, and two bottles of water. They'd no sooner settled down on a bench in the shade several paces away from the Ferris wheel when a lithe brunette approached.

"Justin?" She bent a little at the waist as if she needed to get closer to him to make sure he was the man she was looking for.

Renee volleyed her gaze back to Justin in time to see him flinch. A splash of powdered sugar landed on his jeans, and Renee wanted to brush it away. She fisted her fingers to keep them from touching him.

"Paulette." Justin's gaze flew to Renee, something desperate in the way he looked at her. Renee understood desperation, and her excitement grew. She had a part to play here, and she was certain she'd nail the act.

She allowed herself to reach over and swipe at the sugar on Justin's thigh. He tensed, but she smiled. "This is Paulette?" He'd never detailed his ex's name, but it was clear that the beautiful woman standing before them—wearing a tight pair of jeans, cowboy boots, and a bright pink western shirt—was the woman he'd wanted to show he'd moved on.

"You didn't say she was so pretty." Renee set her barely-touched funnel cake on the bench next to her and clapped her hands together as she stood. "I'm Renee."

Paulette appraised her, and it was very clear that Renee had been found unworthy. Discomfort squirmed through her. She already felt inadequate to be sitting beside Justin, and she didn't need this woman's disdain.

She extended her hand for the cowgirl to shake, which Paulette did with obvious reluctance. Renee almost fell back onto the bench, her confidence completely gone. Justin put his hand on her knee and she curled her fingers around his. Paulette saw every movement, and Renee made a split-second decision. She tucked herself into Justin's side and tilted her head back, stretching up to press a kiss to his cheek.

She refocused on Paulette like she'd just barely realized the other woman hadn't walked away yet. She noted how symmetrical her face was, how bright her eyes, how high her cheekbones. She was several years older than Renee, and she carried her maturity and beauty well. Renee could see why Justin had been with Paulette, and something like a cocktail of jealousy and self-loathing stole through her.

"Are you competing tonight?" Renee asked.

Paulette didn't look away from Justin. "Sure am." She cocked one hip and flashed him a smile that held more than friendship. "You should come see Daisy May."

Renee didn't like the sound of that, but she kept her mouth shut. Justin didn't even attempt to smile. "We'll see if I have time."

Paulette was smart enough to read between the lines, and she nodded, a resigned look on her face. Still, she said, "It was good to see you, Justin," before turning and rejoining another cowgirl who'd been hanging back.

"Good luck tonight!" Renee chirped, and Paulette looked over her shoulder in surprise. Once the women had cleared the area, Justin's chest expanded as he took a full breath.

"Wow." He let the air out in a slow stream.

"Yeah, she's intense. You dated her?"

"Yeah."

"For how long?"

"A couple of years. We ran the rodeo circuit together." He shifted in his seat, and Renee stayed silent—a real feat for her as her mind seemed to whirl at ninety miles a second.

Questions piled up until she finally said, "You must've been serious."

"We were."

"What happened?"

Justin picked up his funnel cake and tore off a bite. "I don't want to talk about it."

Frustration erased the questions from Renee's mind. "That's...fine, I guess." But it wasn't fine. She'd noticed that she spoke much more than Justin did on the phone. He asked her open-ended questions and to tell him about events in her life. She'd happily complied, told him whatever she felt like he'd like to know. Her life volume only had a couple of pages in it, and she was suddenly realizing that Justin's contained a lot more.

"I do want to talk about somethin' else." He gave her a sideways look from under his cowboy hat, pretty much the sexiest thing she'd ever seen.

She swallowed and looked away, the heat from his gaze combined with the summer evening sun, and Renee thought she'd melt at any moment. She picked up her funnel cake, but the fruit topping had soaked into the crispy dough, making it soggy. She tore off a tiny piece on the edge and put it in her mouth.

"Go ahead and talk then," she said.

"I think you were a great assistant." He hung his hands between his knees. "And what you did just now with Paulette was pretty amazing." A haunted smile graced his face. "There was only one flaw."

Renee's defenses flew into place. "Yeah? What's that?"

He turned his head and looked right at her. His blue eyes seared into hers, and his voice came out a bit hoarse when he said, "You missed with your kiss."

He might as well as have poured gasoline into her veins and then lit a match. An instant smile popped onto her face, and she abandoned her funnel cake again. "We should probably fix that for next time."

His right eyebrow cocked. "Next time?"

Feeling brave, and wanting to experience the same things Paulette had, Renee tipped herself forward and hesitated when her forehead collided with Justin's cowboy hat. Only a breath between them, he swept the hat off with one hand and curled the other around her waist.

He closed the distance between them and pressed his lips gently to hers. She drank him in like she hadn't had water in days. Fire flamed through her whole body, and Renee had an inkling that she'd never again experience such a beautiful kiss. And that was one part of being an adult she was very happy about.

CHAPTER 6

Justin enjoyed the fruity taste of Renee's mouth, took his time with the kiss so she'd know his infatuation with her wasn't a whim or something he played around with. She kissed him back with just as much passion, and for the first time since they'd met, he didn't second-guess himself.

He pulled away with a chuckle, sliding his hand along her back and returning his fingers to hers. He squeezed. After clearing the emotion from his throat, he said, "Yeah, you should do that next time. It's real convincing."

Renee giggled beside him, and he now found the sound sexy. She laid her cheek against his shoulder, the ends of her hair tickling his bare bicep. "Well, what about some real dinner?" he asked. "Rodeo's not until eight."

"Dinner sounds great." She picked up her funnel cake, which she'd barely touched. "This got soggy."

"You want another one?"

"Yeah," she deadpanned. "So you can tease me about

eating two bowls of ice cream and then two funnel cakes." She tossed the treat into the trashcan. "No thanks."

"You can have mine." He extended it toward her. "Powdered sugar doesn't sogify anything."

She pinched off a piece and stuck it in her mouth. "Why didn't you eat it?"

He exhaled and gazed into the distance. "Paulette... destroys my appetite." He'd been surprised that Renee had let him off the hook about Paulette. He should tell her that he and Paulette had been engaged, that the woman had left him standing at the altar by himself. He just didn't want to see the sympathy in Renee's eyes. He wanted to see the heat, the fun, the part of himself that he'd lost when he'd had to get a ride back to his cabin-for-one with Ted.

And so he reasoned that it was okay. Renee didn't need to know everything up-front. That was what dating was for. "Hey," he said as they strolled back toward the rodeo grounds, where he'd parked. "The Fourth of July festivities are coming up. I was thinking we should meet up. Go to the fireman's breakfast, or watch the concert in the park, maybe even do the fishing contest."

"First week of July, huh?" She swung their hands between them as they walked, and Justin felt like a five-year-old. He wanted to embrace it, but he just felt silly.

"The festivities run for the whole week before the Fourth," he said. "The grand parade is always on the Fourth."

A troubled look crossed her face, and she remained silent for too long. "What is it?" he asked. If she was the type of woman who couldn't catch a fish, Justin was sunk. He went fishing to *relax*.

He stopped walking, right in the middle of the street. Good thing it was closed. "I'm a terrible kisser, aren't I?" He gave her his best smile, the one he hadn't pulled out in years. It felt good on his face.

She stared at him, horrified, for two heartbeats, and then flung herself into his arms. He twirled her around while they laughed. "Terrible," she said when she sobered. But the blazing inferno in her eyes spoke a different story. She put some distance between them and added, "I just don't know where I'm going to be living come July." She slid him a glance out of the corner of her eye. "That's not a couple of weeks away. That's almost a month away."

The wind went right out of his sails. "So you're saying you'll be moving in less than a month?" His hand in hers suddenly felt too intimate. He wasn't interested in investing his heart and then having the woman leave town in less than thirty days.

"I don't know." She tucked her curls behind her ear. "I haven't revealed some of my biggest flaws."

"Well, let's hear it."

"Let's make a deal," she said.

Justin didn't like the sound of that. "What kind of deal?"

She waited for him to unlock the truck and open her door. She watched him, and he didn't like the weight of it. He finally faced her. "What kind of deal?" he asked again.

She rolled up onto her tiptoes but still couldn't quite reach his eye-height. "I know you have more to say about Paulette. You tell me about her, and I'll tell you about all my flaws."

"*All* of them?"

She stepped up into the truck, smoothing her skirt down her legs, and twisted back to him. "All of them."

Justin slammed the door behind her and took an extra moment before he stepped around the front of the truck. He had so much conflicting information inside. He liked Renee. Talking to her was easy. Kissing her had been fantastic. He still harbored some doubt about if she was the right fit for him. She was flirty and fun. Twenty-four.

He climbed into the cab, thinking maybe he needed to live a little more. Think younger. Be more spontaneous, the way Renee was. "So what are we eating for dinner?"

"Are there any good Chinese places in town?"

Justin lost his appetite, and he decided to be honest about it. "I don't like Chinese food."

"Shut your mouth." Renee looked at him with mock horror.

"You shut yours." He chuckled. "Burgers or fries? I like that. Mexican is great. I'll take pasta over Chinese."

"We had Mexican for lunch."

"One can never have too much chips and salsa."

She giggled. "I can forgive the Chinese food because of the salsa fetish."

"I didn't say I had a fetish."

"Mm hm." She steadfastly looked out her window. "At least I know what to bring you on your birthday. Orange Tic Tacs and chips and salsa."

"The way to a man's heart," Justin said, chuckling even though the flavor combination sounded disgusting. "What about a diner? Breakfast for dinner?"

"Now you're talking. Put bacon on something, and I'm your girl."

The affection he had for her bloomed, expanded, brightened until he admitted to himself that he really liked Renee. Despite him feeling like an old man around her, despite the giggling, despite the previous disaster with her cousin, he really liked Renee Martin.

———

JUSTIN MAY HAVE CONSUMED TOO many French fries at dinner. On top of the greasy funnel cake, and his stomach had him running to the restroom in between the team roping and the bronc riding.

He'd been giving Renee a blow-by-blow of each event, from what was a good score to who the cowboys were. He recognized several of them, as he'd only been out of the circuit for a little over two years.

Bitterness had lingered very close by for most of the evening. He'd taken the job at Brush Creek Ranch in the brief off-season, but he'd never thought he wouldn't rejoin the circuit once he and Paulette were married.

That all changed when she skipped town and never came back. He'd never left again, and most days he didn't regret that his life had gone from winning rodeos to training horses practically overnight. It was the horses he loved anyway. Not the traveling, or the cowgirls, or the late nights under the bright lights.

And he still had horses.

He stopped by the concessions stand on his way back to his seat, sure a soda would calm his stomach. The smell of the hamburgers almost had him running for the bathroom, but he managed to order two sodas and a churro without incident.

The cheers rising from the arena told him the bronc riding was beginning, and he strode back toward the west bleachers and Renee. He'd taken two steps up toward their row when he realized another man had taken his seat.

The man leaned toward Renee, a flirtatious smile on his face. His brown hair was long on one side, and it flopped around like one of the fish Justin liked to catch out on ranch property. The other man was clearly closer to Renee's age, if the boat shoes and V-neck T-shirt were any indication.

Justin blinked, his heart diving down into his already sick stomach. It rebounded, almost choking him as he watched Renee tip her head back and laugh at something the other man had said. He laughed too, and Justin isolated the sounds from the crowd noise, the announcer on the loud speaker, the humming that had started in his head.

Justin turned and went back the way he'd come, dumping the extra soda and the churro in a garbage barrel as he went. He sucked at the soda, his long legs moving fast, trying to get away. But no matter how much carbonation he drank, he knew he'd never erase the sight of the two twenty-something's flirting.

Ten minutes later, his phone rang. Renee's face came up on the screen, and Justin decided to take the call. He was mature enough to have a conversation, especially now that he'd cooled off a little. Finished his soda. Found a quiet place under the blanket of dark sky and sent a prayer toward heaven.

"Hey," he said.

"Where'd you go?" The crowd noise felt chaotic, and Justin just wanted to leave the rodeo. He didn't need to watch one; he'd seen them countless times.

"I needed some fresh air," he said.

Her quick exhalations came through the line. "Liar. This whole place is fresh air. Where are you?"

"I left through the south exit. I'm sitting on some bleachers in the baseball fields across the street."

"I'll be there in a few minutes."

"Suit yourself."

She hung up, and Justin picked her out of the shadows almost as soon as she left the rodeo arena. The stadium lights lit up her Medusa-curls, and a pinch started in Justin's chest. Every step she took made him want to bolt, but he held his position on the top row of bleachers. He'd endured confrontation before, and it was always better to be calm, think rationally not emotionally.

An image of that other man flipping his long hair passed through Justin's mind just as Renee stepped onto the grass. She lifted her hand and he returned the gesture. Her footsteps made metallic sounds as she climbed the steps. She didn't hesitate in her approach and sat right next to him on the bench.

She heaved out a heavy breath. "It's dark out here."

"Lots of room to think."

"What do you need to think about?"

Justin turned and looked right at her. "Us."

A smile flickered across her face, but it only stuck for a few seconds. She rubbed her hands up and down her arms as if she were cold, but though the sun had gone down, it definitely wasn't that chilly.

"I saw that guy flirting with you," he said, the words nearly sticking in his throat. "You guys looked like you were gettin' along real well." He lifted his soda straw to his lips but lowered it when he found the cup empty.

"He just sat down and started talking," Renee said. "He...." She clamped her lips shut and looked out over the navy baseball field.

"He was probably nice," Justin said. "Funny. Charming. He ask you out?"

"I don't want to talk about it."

Justin chuckled darkly. "Nice try. We're already talkin' about it."

"You didn't tell me hardly anything about Paulette." When she looked at him again, accusations swam in her eyes.

"You didn't tell me all your flaws either." Looking into her face, some of the fight inside him died. "You should probably go out with him," he said, his voice tired now. "He's more your age."

She blinked, her face blanching. Questions ran through her expression, then understanding. "So that's what you're worried about."

"I'm quite a bit older than you."

"Then you should be handling this in a more mature way."

Justin shook his head. "I'm not handling it well, Renee, because I like you quite a lot. More than I probably should after only seeing you a couple of times."

"We talk a lot on the phone." Her voice sounded higher than normal.

He reached for her hand, unable to stop himself. "*You* talk a lot on the phone."

She giggled but cut the sound off after only a moment. "So you kinda like me, huh?"

"I don't go around kissing every woman I see."

Her fingers tightened around his. "Eight years isn't that big of a deal."

"Enough to be in a different generation," he said. His tongue felt thick, but he knew he needed to say more. "I'm also not handling it well, because my last girlfriend, well, she wasn't just my girlfriend."

His chin faced the ground, but Renee slid her fingers beneath his face and lifted it toward hers. Compassion swam in her gorgeous eyes, and Justin wanted to dive in too. "Were you married?"

"Almost."

"We got interrupted last time I asked you this. Have you ever been married?"

"No."

"Engaged?"

"Twice."

She sucked in a breath. "Wow."

"How many boyfriends have you had?" he asked.

"One."

Disbelief tore through Justin. "One boyfriend? Ever?"

"I'm fairly invisible to most men." She removed her hand from his and wound her fingers around each other, a tale-tell sign of her nerves. "Even you looked right past me the first time we met."

"I did not."

"You completely ignored me."

"I saw you, I just didn't want to get involved."

Her voice sounded hollow when she said, "Because of Leah, right?"

"Definitely because of Leah."

"What happened with you guys?"

"Nothing." Justin sighed. "I saw you, Renee. It would be pretty impossible not to see you." He reached over and tucked one of her curls behind her ear, where it just popped out again. "And I'm obviously not the only one. Who comes over to a woman at a rodeo and just sits down like she's not with someone?"

"You have nothing to worry about." Her gaze heated the longer she looked at him.

"Oh no?"

She shook her head slowly, seductively. Renee leaned closer and Justin smiled. "Maybe you need to prove it. I know that other guy asked you out. I'm asking you: Will you go with me to the Fourth of July festivities in Brush Creek?"

A shy smile touched her mouth. "Yes, of course."

Justin leaned forward and brushed his lips against hers. A barely-there touch that ignited a firestorm in his blood. "What did you tell that other guy?"

CHAPTER 7

Renee's heartbeat froze in her chest, but because it was a strong muscle, it broke through the ice and continued pumping. She'd been surprised when Alvin had plopped himself next to her at the rodeo. He seemed interested, and Renee wouldn't lie—it had felt nice. Nice to be seen. Nice to be noticed among the hundreds of people at the rodeo. Nice to be flirted with.

"He asked if I liked ice cream."

Justin straightened and laughed, a full sound that painted the sky. Renee liked the way it made her feel like pure joy existed in the world and she wanted to hear his laugh every day if she could.

"Of course I said yes. I mean, it's ice cream. Who doesn't like ice cream?"

"Oh, I suppose the lactose intolerant don't like ice cream."

"Oh, they do," Renee insisted. "I had a lactose intolerant roommate in college who'd eat two bowls of caramel pecan after every semester, knowing full well she'd be sick for twenty-four hours afterward."

Justin's eyes rounded for a moment before crinkling in the corners. "You still haven't answered my question."

Renee appreciated the jealousy, but she wished she didn't. It made her feel immature, and she didn't want to act like she was eight years younger than Justin. Or like she was in junior high and needed boys fighting over her. At the same time, she'd never experienced a man being jealous over her before. Her.

"I told him I was really sorry, but that I was seeing someone."

A smile burst across his face. "Is that what we're doing? Seeing each other?"

"Well, if *one* of us didn't work so much, we'd probably be able to see enough of each other to be considered dating." She giggled at the mock surprise on his face, and nudged him with her shoulder.

He pulled her into his chest and kept her close. She matched her breathing to his, and breathed in the solace of sitting in the silence with Justin's arm around her. She didn't want anything to break this moment, but all too soon, he said, "All right, gorgeous. Time to go."

She basked in the warmth of the endearment, kept her hand tucked in his, and enjoyed every moment of the drive back to Brush Creek.

———

AFTER ONLY THE fourth day on the job, Renee decided for sure that she hated her position with Dinosaur National

Monument. The best part was Delilah, a plus-size woman a few years older than Renee. They'd bonded over day-old doughnuts during a break on Renee's first shift. She worked in the gift shop, and they were on the same schedule, so when Renee pushed into the staff room—blessedly air conditioned, something the entrance booth was not—the best part of her day became when she saw Delilah standing at the head of the table with a Cinnabon.

"Is that for me?" Renee stopped short, her hopes soaring as high as the clouds.

"Mine's in the microwave." Delilah extended the pastry box toward Renee, who swept toward her and engulfed her in a hug.

"Thank you." She took the box and didn't bother with the microwave. "It has been a day already. I got yelled at because someone's annual pass had expired. Like it's my fault it's June, or that I set the prices for entrance."

Delilah shook her head. "I bet they were mad they couldn't get the senior citizen discount too."

"Yes!" Renee threw her hands into the air. "Sorry, but fifty-seven isn't a senior citizen." She forked off a piece of cinnamon roll and stuck it in her mouth. She moaned.

"It's better warm," Delilah said, flipping her black braids over her shoulder before digging into her own treat. "How's Justin?"

Renee's muscles didn't seem strong enough to hold her up while speaking of him. "He's dreamy," she sighed. "What about Sherman?"

A twinkle entered Delilah's eye. "I think he's going to propose soon."

Renee squealed around a healthy bite of carbs and frosting. "De*li*-lah! Really?" If Justin heard her tone, he'd cringe. Renee dismissed the nagging thought of how immature she was, as if he was this wise sage.

"I saw a receipt from a jeweler." She got up and pulled a salad from the fridge. "But he walked in right after that, and I couldn't snoop anymore."

"Well, dig around some more tonight. I want details." Renee found it ironic that she ate a salad for lunch—after consuming a cinnamon roll. At least she ate something green. Renee generally avoided anything in the plant family, as the thickness of her midsection testified.

The conversation moved on to work, to Delilah's mother, who was in the hospital after surgery, to Renee's housing situation.

"So are you going to move closer?" Delilah asked.

Renee scraped the tines of the fork along the bottom of the now-empty cinnamon roll box. "I don't know."

"Things must be more serious than 'dreamy' with Justy-Justington." Delilah sang the nickname, which elicited a smile from Renee.

"It's complicated."

"How so?"

"I don't see him very often. Only twice, actually. We're meeting up again in a few weeks."

Delilah paused with a forkful of baby spinach halfway to her mouth. "You don't see him? The ranch can't be that far from your place."

"Maybe fifteen minutes."

"Why don't you go up there and see him?"

"He hasn't ever invited me to."

"Oh, honey." Delilah patted Renee's hand in a grandmotherly fashion. "You don't need an invitation, especially if you take food."

Chips and salsa, Renee thought. "You really think I can just show up unannounced?"

Delilah shrugged. "If you're interested in him, I don't see why not."

A sliver of discomfort pressed into her heart. "I'm interested in him. I'm just not sure he's quite as interested in me."

"Only you can know that." Delilah stood. "Well, duty calls. See you Thursday." She bent down and gave Renee a hug before she headed out the door. Thoughts of Justin's jealousy flooded her memory, and she got up and tossed her garbage in the trashcan.

Justin liked her. He'd said so right out loud. Renee wasn't sure why she doubted it, doubted herself. As she took the golf cart back out to the entrance booth—the sun beating down on the red rocks, the black highways, everything with a fervor—she made a commitment to herself that she wouldn't live so much inside her self-doubt. Not anymore.

Several days later, she darkened the doorway of the church again, this time wearing a black and blue maxi dress. Leah minced behind her in shoes with tiny pinpoint heels and straps that cut into the tops of her feet. But, apparently, there was a new bachelor in town, and Leah didn't want to miss her chance to make a first impression.

Renee had argued for a solid thirty minutes that a fishmonger—in the middle of western Utah—was nothing to get excited about. Even if he was rumored to have delicious, dark hair and muscles from wrestling sixty-pound fish all day.

She'd have gone to church anyway; it was the one place where she never felt out of place, never felt overlooked, never wanted to hide.

This Sabbath was no different. Pastor Peters spoke about finding the qualities of Christ and trying to emulate them. He spoke about the Savior's undying love for those around Him, and Renee's heart expanded and warmed.

She felt loved when she was at church, despite Leah's constant head-swinging. The sermon ended, and Renee leaned toward her cousin. "Maybe he's not religious."

"Don't be ridiculous." Leah grinned, looking very much like a wolf after her next meal. "All small towns revolve around a church, whether the people are religious or not." She stood, her gaze sweeping the crowd. "Besides. There he is." She strutted away, and Renee suddenly realized why Justin avoided Leah if possible. Did she look like her cousin? Wearing a too-tight dress, ridiculous heels, too much lipstick?

She self-consciously ran her fingers across her lips. "You okay?"

The male voice startled her, and she jumped as she turned, nearly throwing out her back in the process. There stood tall, dark, and dreamy Justin Jackman. Every nerve in her body fired on all cylinders. "Hey."

"Hey, yourself," he said in the same playful, flirty tone.

"I've never seen you at church."

"I don't always have Sundays off." He offered her his elbow, and she laced her hand through it.

"Did you come down alone?"

"Sure did." He leaned down and pressed his warm mouth to her temple. "Was hopin' to see you. Maybe we could go to the park or something."

"I have stuff to make sandwiches," she said. "We could stop by my place first."

He darted a glance in the direction Leah had gone. "Will your cousin be home?"

"I'll meet you at the park." She smiled at him so he'd know it was okay if he didn't come back to the house with her. "Oh, and I do have an appointment at four o'clock."

"An appointment on Sunday?"

Renee's nerves bounced again, this time for a different reason. "I'm moving out," she said. "I'm looking at a house for rent at the base of the canyon." She wasn't sure what meaning she wanted him to hear in the words, but he definitely heard something as his eyebrows nearly disappeared under his sexy cowboy hat.

"You're staying here?"

"I don't like my job much anyway, and I do like you, so I thought maybe I'd stick closer to Brush Creek for a while." It was one of the most adult things she'd ever done, and pride swelled beneath her breastbone.

"Are you going to quit your job with the National Parks?"

"I'm looking into a couple of other options," she said.

"Like what?"

Her stomach growled. "Let's talk about it at the park, okay?" She glanced toward Leah. "Besides, here comes Leah."

That got Justin moving, and Renee laughed as he practically ran from the chapel.

"Was that Justin?" Leah asked.

"Sure was. I'm taking sandwiches to the park, so can we go?" She tossed a look to where the fishmonger still stood with a gaggle of girls surrounding him. "How was the new guy?"

Leah grinned again. "I got his number, so it's definitely time to go." She walked out without looking back, and Renee appreciated her cousin's determination.

A half an hour later, she arrived at Oxbow Park, the sky so blue above her head that it seemed surreal. She hadn't changed out of the maxi dress, because it was the most comfortable piece of clothing she owned. She liked the way it swished around her legs, and she liked the glint in Justin's eyes when he caught sight of her. He rose from the bench where he'd been sitting.

"Wow, a picnic basket and everything." He glanced at the basket she carried, complete with a red-and-white checkered tablecloth peeking out the top.

"I don't mess around." She handed him the basket and slipped her hand into the crook of his arm again. "Where do you want to go?"

Oxbow Park was one of her favorite spots, with a river running down the edge of it. A large pond sat on the other end, with an island in the middle of it. Two bridges went out to the island, which was often crowded with families on the weekends.

A running path circled the park, and there were three separate pavilions for larger gatherings. The grass glittered like emeralds in the sun, and Justin smartly stuck to the shade of the larger trees that filled the park.

As they moved away from the parking lot and the street,

it was almost like they'd stepped from city to forest. A lazy breeze whispered through the trees, and the faint scent of a campfire wafted toward them.

"I called my parents this weekend," he said.

It took all she had not to look at him. "How are they?"

"Alive and kickin'." He scuffed his boots along the path. "My dad owns a machine repair shop there. Ma bakes too much. She said I need to come home so I can try her peach pie." He chuckled.

"Did you tell her you don't like warm fruit?"

"She knows. That's why she said that." He pointed to a bend in the river, where a single picnic table sat empty. "What about right here?"

"Looks good." She took out the tablecloth and spread it into place. She pulled out a container of pasta salad she'd made the night before, as well as a loaf of bread, sliced turkey and cheese, and a travel-size bottle of mayo. With one ripe tomato sliced and ready, Justin placed a stack of paper plates and a roll of paper towels in the middle of the table.

Rene lifted two bags of chips from the picnic basket and a six-pack of soda. "I hope you like orange," she said. "It's not quite like a Tic Tac, but I thought it would suffice."

He plucked a can from the plastic ring and studied it like he could taste it just by looking. "I can't say I've ever had an orange soda."

"Even as a child?"

"We didn't have a lot of money growing up. My parents didn't buy soda." He popped the top, the satisfying fizz of carbonation filling the air. "Smells good." He threw back a few swallows. She watched and waited for his reaction. He smacked his lips a couple of times, a completely adorable action Renee committed to memory. He met her eye. "It's delicious." He drained the whole can while Renee giggled.

He set the empty can on the picnic table and leaned into his palm. He lifted his leg and planted it on the other side of Renee, effectively trapping her. "You want a taste?"

"Mm hm." She closed her eyes and tilted her head back to receive his kiss. His mouth was cold and tasted like oranges, with a little bit of bubbly left over. She was aware of his hands on her back, then the side of her face, and then she lost all reason as he deepened their kiss.

He pulled away, and Renee kept her eyes closed as she tried to regulate her breathing.

"You're beautiful," he whispered, brushing her curls away from her face. They settled right back against her cheeks the way they always did, and his fingers trailed down her neck and over her shoulders. "Should we eat?"

She opened her eyes, and the sun seemed ten times brighter than before. She felt cherished under the gaze of this man, and she'd never felt like that before. She smiled up at him and said, "Yeah, I'm starving."

Renee spread mayo on two pieces of bread and layered on turkey and muenster. "Would you like to come with me to look at the house?"

He dropped the plastic knife he'd been using, his eyes flying to hers. "You want me to come look at the house with you?"

"Yes." She'd asked on a whim, but she could see how serious this was to him. It probably should've been to her too. She chalked it up to one of their generational differences. She, a carefree millennial who did what she felt like without much thought. He, on the cusp of Generation X, who'd learned to work hard and take life seriously. Go after what he wanted with determination, creativity, and hard work. If something didn't work for Renee, she tried something else. She didn't stick with it.

And she wanted to stick with Justin. She'd made a decision to do just that by choosing to stay in Brush Creek.

He finished putting together his sandwich and ripped open a bag of chips, dumping a healthy portion onto his plate. "So the house is at the base of the canyon. I must drive by it every time I come down from the ranch."

"I'm sure you do." She thumbed on her phone and pulled up the listing. "It's this one." She showed him the phone, which displayed a cute little blue bungalow, white shutters on the windows, a front porch that had enough room for two chairs and a small round table between them, and a small yard. One tall tree dominated the front yard, and there wasn't a full garage, only a carport.

He studied it for a few seconds, taking the phone and swiping down to read more about it. "Looks nice, Renee." He handed the phone back with a gentle smile she could lose her heart to if she wasn't careful.

She took the phone and turned her back on him, her heart suddenly thundering against her ribcage. Had she already lost a piece of her heart to him? Had she given it to him willingly? She wanted to, and that scared her more than anything.

Renee took a bite of her sandwich, hoping to calm the quaking in her stomach with food. And later, she'd need to call her mother to find out what falling in love felt like.

"He's right behind me," she said into her phone, her voice hushed like he could overhear her from inside another car.

"Well, honey, do you like him?"

"Of course I do, Mom. Can't you hear how much I'm freaking out?"

"All right," her mother said in the tone she used when she was trying to calm Renee down. "It's only been a few weeks. Nothing has to be decided right now."

"Right. Of course." She pulled into the driveway at the blue bungalow, Justin only seconds behind her. "So just play it cool."

Her mom laughed. "Honey, be you. That's it. You'll know what to do and when to do it if you trust yourself."

"Mom," she whined. "I don't know how to do that."

Justin got out of his truck, and a blip of panic flipped through Renee. "I have to go, Mom. Just tell me one more thing. How did you know Dad was the one for you?"

"The same way you knew Russell wasn't."

Renee ended the call just as Justin reached her window, the name of the one boyfriend she'd had in college ringing in her ears. Her mom was right. She'd liked Russell, but there had been no spark.

One look at Justin, and an entire fireworks show filled the space between them. She got out of the car and glanced around the yard. The grass needed to be trimmed, and weeds had started to take over in some spots. The flowerbeds hadn't been planted this year, but the oak tree stood guard over all of it with a fierce protection Renee could feel.

She felt small under its branches, but she liked it. She turned to Justin. "I like this place."

"You haven't even been inside yet."

"It feels good."

He chuckled and tucked her hand into his. "You can't rent a place because of how you feel standing on the front lawn."

"Maybe not someone as old as you can," she said, pushing away from him with a squeal when he protested. "But I can." She bounded up the front steps just as the door opened.

The realtor stepped out, a smile on her face. "Renee, good to see you." The two women shook hands. "And you brought Justin Jackman." A strange look crossed the woman's face, and Renee turned around to judge Justin's reaction.

He didn't give one. Simply stepped next to Renee, took her hand in his again, and said, "Mya."

Renee had forgotten that everyone knew everyone else in Brush Creek. She was the newcomer, the outsider, the one still trying to figure out the community.

Mya recovered quickly, and Renee wanted to know the basis of her shock at seeing Justin, and gestured them into the house. The floors were new, the paint too. Granite countertops had just been installed, and the kitchen housed all new appliances. The backyard was twice as big as the front—a bit of a disappointment as Renee wasn't exactly an outdoorsy person. Her idea of a fun afternoon was lying on the couch, reading.

"So, just let me know," Mya said once the tour had finished.

Renee stood on the back porch, the scent of Justin's cologne clogging her nose. She wanted to be where he was, wanted to see how far this relationship could go.

"I want it." She turned back to Mya. "When can I move in?"

Justin's arm slid around her waist. "You sure?" he murmured, his breath skating across her ear and neck.

"I'm sure." She saw the way Mya catalogued the way Justin kneaded Renee closer, and she wondered what he was doing. He'd never seemed possessive of her previously, and she didn't like being used in some game between locals.

You're going to be a local, she told herself.

"Great." Mya started through the house. "I'll grab the paperwork from my car and be right back."

Renee waited until she heard the front door close, and then she glanced at Justin. "What's with you and her?"

"Nothing."

"You say that so much when it isn't true." She peered at him. "How many women have you dated in this town?"

"Hardly any," he said. "I swear," he added when she cocked her hip and gave him a dubious look.

"She seemed surprised to see you here."

"I don't get off the ranch much."

Pieces clicked around her head. "So you blew her off by saying you couldn't leave the ranch."

Justin sighed. "She wanted to go out with me only a few months after Paulette." He stepped into the house too. "I didn't want to hurt her, but I wasn't dating at the time."

Renee followed him. "Who have you dated since Paulette?"

He paused with one hand on the doorknob. He turned halfway back to her, his head bent down so she couldn't really see his face beneath his cowboy hat. "Just you, Renee." He opened the door and stepped out into the sunlight.

Renee let him go, because she had no idea what to make of him. A man like him hadn't dated in two years? And not because women hadn't tried. She wondered what about her had attracted his attention, and how she could possibly maintain his interest when so many other, prettier, women hadn't been able to.

CHAPTER 8

Justin spent his Monday in the fields, with horses in the arena, and then all evening unloading Renee's boxes into her new house. He worked methodically, ignoring the tightness in his muscles. Her quick smile sent his pain and exhaustion running for the hills anyway.

His feelings for her surprised him, and he'd been obsessing over their depth since yesterday at Oxbow Park. It had been quite possibly the best afternoon he'd spent with a woman, ever. With anyone.

Renee's new house sat nine minutes from his cabin. He'd timed it on his way down to help her move in. He could see her every night if he wanted to. And he wanted to. So much that he didn't think he'd be able to keep himself up at the horse ranch when she was only nine minutes away.

He set down the last box and pulled out his container of Tic Tacs. They wouldn't satiate the hunger gnawing at him, but he downed a handful anyway. Renee came in from the backyard wearing a pair of cutoffs that got his blood racing every time he looked at her.

"Got any of those for me?" She paused close enough for him to catch a whiff of her perfume. He told himself not to fall so fast, but Justin couldn't seem to stop himself.

He handed her the container. "That was the last box. Can I take you to dinner?"

She ate the rest of his Tic Tacs and tossed the empty container into an empty box she was using as a trashcan. "Sure."

"Do you mind driving a bit?"

She approached him and slid both hands up his chest. "How far?"

He kissed her, his need for her stronger than his need for food. Justin pulled back sooner than he would've liked. "Not far. Beaverton has an Italian restaurant I think you'll like."

"Trying to sweeten me up with pasta?"

"Will that work?"

She laughed and he enjoyed the feel of her next to him while she experienced such joy. "I think it'll actually work, yeah."

"Well, let's go then."

———

LUNCHTIME THE FOLLOWING day found Justin on the back of his horse, a sandwich in one hand and a bottle of Gatorade in the other. The sun beat down on the landscape around him, and his cowboy hat did little to ease the blinding light.

He'd escaped the rigorous schedule on the ranch, at least for an hour. He hadn't checked with Walker. Justin would get his work done; he always did. He rarely needed a break, but today, he felt emotionally overwhelmed.

After another late night, and after hours of lying in bed without sleeping, Justin couldn't deny how he felt about Renee. Once he'd accepted it, sleep had come instantly.

His phone buzzed and chimed, and Justin pulled it out of his shirt pocket.

Renee: Quit my job today.

Justin's heart tripped over itself. You did?

Renee: Yeah. I'm going to miss my friend, but I can't stand in that booth for another second.

Justin: Gotta listen to your gut.

Renee: I'm still working for the National Parks Department.

Justin: Yeah?

Renee: Yeah. I'm going to be the social media coordinator for the monument.

Justin stared at the phone, seeing the words but not comprehending them. What did a social media coordinator even do?

Renee: You know, like twitter, Facebook, instagram, stuff like that.

Justin: I actually have no idea about most of that.

When he was in the rodeo, his manager had set up a twitter account for him, but Justin had never even logged in. His manager had taken care of all of that, and Justin didn't know if the account even existed anymore.

Renee: I get to work from home.

Justin: That's the best commute.

Renee: Sure is.

Justin turned his face into the wind, steering his horse toward the butte. Peppercorn had a pelt of off-white that looked like someone had spilled an entire container of pepper across her back, thus the name. Justin had raised her from a colt, and she'd taken him to victory as a heeler horse the last two years of his rodeo career.

He whistled between his teeth when he realized he hadn't seen his dog for a while. Movement in the sagebrush up ahead caught his attention, and Roy came bounding back. His tongue lolled out of his mouth as Justin drained the last of his sports drink.

He sighed. "So, boy. What do you think I should do about Renee?"

Roy looked at him with eagerness, his tail wagging his whole body.

"Yeah, I'm being stupid about nothing." And the words sounded one-hundred percent true. So he released his worries and let God lead the horse to the shade. He believed God would lead him too, if he'd let go of the reins and exercise his faith.

He also knew that was easier said than done, but he was determined to try.

————

THE WEEKS PASSED in a blur of sun and wind and horses and spending a couple of hours in the evenings with Renee. She never ventured up the canyon, something Justin didn't notice until she brought it up.

She brought up everything, it seemed. Her brothers and

sisters. Her friends. Her jobs over the years. What had happened in town that day, what the pastor had said at church, what the neighbors were gossiping about.

Justin pulled up to her house on Friday evening and got out of his truck. She met him on the front porch with her shoulder bag slung across her body. "You ready for this concert?"

"It's not gonna get wild or anything. It's bluegrass." He watched shock travel across her face. "I can see you didn't know that."

"You said it was a concert."

Justin laughed and swept an arm around her waist. "There will be live people playing instruments. It *is* a concert."

She glared up at him, straining against his grip. "What kind of instruments?"

"Banjos and guitars. Probably a keyboard."

"I feel like you should've been more clear." She glanced down at her knee-length skirt. "I'm going to go change."

"Probably a good idea," he called after her, though he enjoyed the view with the skirt. "We have to sit on the ground."

She spun back to him, her eyes practically on fire. "What?"

"It's a concert *in the park*. I know I told you that." He entered her house and let the door settle closed behind him. "It's like you don't know where you live. It's *Brush Creek*," he said. "Small town America."

She lifted her chin and turned the corner to go into her bedroom. "I know," she called back to him.

Justin chuckled as he sank onto her couch. He leaned

back, all the knots in his muscles unwinding. It had been a long week of work, and he didn't have a day off for nine more days. He'd never minded, but he hadn't dated anyone since he'd moved to Brush Creek. He was finding it hard to maintain a relationship and keep up with all the work on the ranch.

"Justin?" His name echoed in his mind, and he tried to locate it. Whiteness blanketed everything about him, and his head swam.

Someone touched his arm, and he jerked, his fist colliding with something hard and soft at the same time.

His eyes snapped open at the same time Renee cried out. Justin blinked, realizing in a single moment that he'd fallen asleep—and punched his girlfriend in the eye.

"Renee," he said, pulling at her hands, which covered her left eye. "Let me see. I'm so sorry."

Both of her eyes watered, her makeup clearly high quality because it didn't run. She couldn't keep her eye open for long, and it fluttered closed again.

Regret lanced through him, and he cursed his exhaustion. "I'm sorry," he said again.

She tried to laugh, but he could tell it wasn't genuine. "So you're a bad waker-upper." She smiled, but Justin could only see half of it as she kept her eye covered with her hands. "Noted."

"I'm a sleepwalker too," he said. "My mom used to put a baby gate in the hallway so I wouldn't fall down the stairs."

She slowly lowered her hands. "You're adorable," she said.

Justin ducked his head, pleasure flowing through him.

Though she seemed to like kissing him, she hadn't really paid him any compliments. He'd tried to tell her she was beautiful whenever he got the chance, whether through texts, calls, or in person.

He cleared his throat. "So did I sleep through the concert?"

"I may have taken a little long changing," she said. "But it's only been about twenty minutes."

He lifted his eyes to hers, glad that hers only looked a little red. "How's your eye? We don't have to go."

"It's my first holiday in Brush Creek. I want to go." She covered his hand with both of hers. "I want to go with you."

A tremor of fear passed through Justin. He didn't understand it. A few days ago, he'd released his concerns and determined to trust in the Lord. But actually having to do it took more courage than Justin thought he had.

"Let's go," he said, standing and heading toward the front door. He needed to put some distance between him and Renee until he could figure out why she scared him.

They arrived at the park later than he'd planned so there wasn't anywhere to park in the lot. He found a spot a few blocks away and they walked hand-in-hand to the concert. He carried two blankets and a flashlight. Renee didn't bring anything but her cell phone, which she couldn't seem to look away from.

Annoyance sang through him as he spread one blanket on the ground and let her settle onto it.

"Who you talking to?" he finally asked.

A few seconds passed before she even looked up. "One of

my sisters. Remember I told you about Julia? She's having some trouble with her boyfriend." She focused on the phone again, and Justin tried to enjoy the bluegrass band on the stage. But they were a little too far away to appreciate the skill it took to strum a banjo, and Justin felt his attention wandering.

His own phone rested in his back pocket, silent. The only person who ever texted or called sat beside him, worlds away. Well, Walker sent him messages everyday too, but Justin didn't want to talk about horses or balers.

Darkness started to fall, and Justin's muscles twitched to leave. He stood and stretched his legs, making sure Renee noticed him. When she didn't say anything, Justin strode toward the bright lights of the pavilion, where he'd find something to drink and maybe some of the bakery's famous chocolate chip cookies.

He found Doug Munk, the owner of the bakery, but no cookies. He bypassed the orange soda in favor of a diet cola, where he also found a sliver of baklava still on a slip of waxed paper. He devoured the treat in two bites, the crisp puff pastry melting against his tongue. Still, he wasn't a huge fan of honey, and the dessert didn't satisfy the way he wanted it to.

He feared nothing would except the woman he'd left on the blanket. The woman who didn't even know he was gone.

"Hey, Justin."

He glanced up to find Mya standing only a pace away, her golden hair gleaming under the artificial lights. She wore a smile that suggested more than friendliness, and Justin found himself returning it.

She flipped open her soda and took a sip of it. "Are you liking the band?"

Justin couldn't really say, so he just shrugged. "I've always liked bluegrass."

"I grew up playing the fiddle." She sighed as she moved to his side and leaned against a pillar. She faced the stage, but it was far enough away that only the faintest warblings of music could be heard.

"No kidding," Justin said. "My dad taught me and my brothers the guitar."

"So we're half of a bluegrass band already."

Justin nodded. "Guess so."

"You still have that dog?"

"The one you thought was—what did you call him? A terror?" He chuckled, remembering that day in the park, almost two years ago. Roy had been leashed and everything. He hadn't barked. "He just wanted your ball."

"I wish you would've told me that at the time."

"You dropped it when you scampered away from him, screaming."

"I wasn't screaming." She slapped him in the chest, and her hand struck him emotionally as well. What was he doing? Flirting with another woman?

He glanced at Mya and found her light blue eyes locked on him. "So tell me what's goin' on between you and Renee Martin." Mya spoke with an even tone, her face giving away nothing. Justin liked her western twang, liked that she wore a pair of jeans and a pink pair of cowgirl boots. She fit in Brush Creek. She could probably fit with him.

"We're dating." He spoke with the same level voice and kept his eyes on hers. He wasn't embarrassed of his relationship with Renee. He just didn't quite know how to quantify it.

"Is she here tonight?" Mya looked around like she should be on Justin's arm.

"Yeah," he said.

Mya raised her hand and trailed her fingers along his collar. "Too bad." She sauntered away, pausing at the edge of the cement and glancing back at him. Her eyes held blue fire that Justin felt all the way down into his stomach.

CHAPTER 9

Renee's thumbs flew across her phone as she tried to help her sister through her boyfriend crisis. When she finally glanced up, she realized she had a crisis of her own, because Justin had disappeared.

She couldn't be sure how long he'd been gone, though she vaguely remembered him getting up and saying something.

Around her, people were standing and folding blankets. Panic raced through her bloodstream as she scrambled to her feet too. Her phone went off again, but she ignored it. The second blanket Justin had brought sat in the corner of the first, and the flashlight lay in the center. She glanced around, noting the pain in her left eye. She cringed when she thought about what it might look like by the time she got home.

Her heart thundered like a herd of galloping horses. She spun in a circle, looking for Justin. She didn't see him anywhere. As the crowd thinned, she realized she was in real trouble. Perhaps he'd left her here completely.

She dismissed the idea almost as quickly as it had come, angry the thought was even there. But it was. Renee still struggled to believe Justin wanted to be with her, despite his frequent declarations of her beauty, despite the affectionate way he looked at her when they were alone, despite the fire between them when they kissed.

Renee pulled out the only weapon she had: her phone. She dialed Justin, desperate to hear his voice on the other end of the line.

"Hello?"

She hated the way he said it like he didn't know who was calling. He never answered the phone like that. Never.

"Hey," she said, a giggle tacking itself onto the end. "Where are you? The concert is over."

"I know."

"So you're still here?"

"Sittin' in my truck, waiting for you."

She turned in a circle again, unsure of which way to go. Julia had texted on the drive over, and well, Renee hadn't really been paying attention.

"You know," he said. "When you said you wanted to go to the concert with me, I believed you."

"I did," she said, exhaling. "It's just that Julia—she's my most needy sister, and—" She bent and picked up the blanket that hadn't been used. "I'm sorry." She tossed the flashlight onto the blanket and folded the one she'd been sitting on. "I'll be right there." She hung up, because she thought she might cry and she didn't want him to witness that for a second time in only one night.

Almost everyone was heading back past the stage, and she remembered coming past the musicians when they'd arrived. She followed them, picking out landmarks though it was dark now. She reached the street and headed north, hoping she was right. Cars lined the street in that direction, so she figured she was safe.

Sure enough, after a few blocks, Justin's big silver truck came into view. He sat inside, his cowboy hat pushed low over his face.

Renee tossed the blankets in the back and went around to the passenger side, her insides jiggling like someone had set them in gelatin. At the same time, her frustration fumed. Would it have been so hard for him to come meet her? Make sure she made it the three blocks from the park?

She tried to open the door, but it was locked. Inside the truck, Justin startled and pushed his hat back. He caught sight of her and he unlocked the truck so she could get in. She climbed in and secured her seat belt, her tongue suddenly too thick to fit in her mouth.

Justin drove, just as silent. After only a block, Renee blurted, "I'm sorry, okay? You didn't have to leave me there."

"You left me a while ago, sweetheart."

She hated the endearment when said so sarcastically. "I don't know how to fix this."

Justin stayed silent until he pulled into her driveway. He put the truck in park and turned to face her. "I understand your sister needed you. I do. I just—I felt like a fool sitting there by myself."

"I'll put my phone away next time."

He remained quiet, and in Renee's experience, that was never good. "Talk to me. What are you thinking about?"

"Us."

A smile flashed across her face. "So there's still an us?"

"I know a couple of people who would like it if there weren't."

Her stomach flipped. "Are you one of them?"

He finally looked at her, and she fell into his ocean-colored eyes. "No." He reached out and brushed his fingertips along her collarbone in a gesture that made her skin hum and her muscles shiver. "Fireman's breakfast in the morning?"

She nodded. "I'll leave my phone at home." She slid across the seat and pressed a kiss to his lips, glad when he received her willingly. "I really am sorry," she whispered against his lips.

"Kiss me again so I can be sure."

She giggled before happily complying with his request.

———

THE FOLLOWING MORNING, Renee rose long before she normally did. She squeezed herself into a pair of yoga pants she swore hadn't been so tight the last time she'd worn them. She secured her hair out of her face with several barrettes and headed toward Main Street, where she'd learned that a women's workout class was held every morning at six a.m.

She'd never given much thought to her extra weight, besides noticing she had it and some other women didn't. She liked to eat, and she liked sweets, and she didn't mind that her clothes were in the double-digits for size.

But she'd experienced the way Justin lived, and he liked to move. He hiked, and he fished, and he worked constantly. He'd never said a single thing to her about coming with him on any of those activities, but she'd like to spend more time with him, and she thought the first step would be to get in shape.

Trepidation tripped through her when she pulled into the lot and found it mostly full. She didn't know many people in town, and she wasn't particularly chipper this early in the morning. She told herself this was a great way to make new friends, and she pushed through the door and into the center.

Gym equipment lined the far wall, leaving the rest of the large room open. Black mats had been fitted together to create a softer floor, and at least two dozen women loitered in small groups, chattering. None of them seemed to know the sun had barely risen.

Renee shifted one way, then the next, her eye catching on her realtor's. The way Mya had appraised her once she'd seen Justin flashed through Renee's mind, but she headed in that direction anyway.

"Hey, Mya." She put on a smile she hoped looked normal.

"Renee." She returned the smile, but it was short lived and low on actual happiness to see Renee. "This is Joy and Valerie. They live down the street from me."

Renee grinned and shook hands with the women, one blonde-haired and one on the mousy side of brown. "Where do you guys live?"

"Over in Pheasant Springs," Joy said, like Renee should know where that was. She nodded like she did.

"Renee just moved into Canyon Glen," Mya said. "One of the older homes that was incorporated into the new lots."

Joy, the blonde who certainly didn't eat more than a single bite of ice cream, seemed interested. "Oh, do you like it? I used to live in Canyon Glen."

"It's wonderful," Renee said, keeping the bit about how this was the first place she'd ever lived on her own under her tongue. "I think I'm going to paint the outside a different color, but other than that, I like it."

Mya tilted her head to the side, her dark curls falling over her shoulder despite the ponytail she'd pulled them into. "You don't like the blue?"

"I—" Renee cut off when Joy's hand landed on her arm. "You live in the blue bungalow?"

Renee took in the interest in her eyes, the sparkle almost as bright as the one she'd seen in Justin's eyes when he spoke about the rodeo. "Yeah, I just moved in a couple of weeks ago."

"I used to live there." Joy grinned, and Renee basked in the genuine comfort of it. "We put in the garden spot in the back the first year we were married." She turned when the instructor called out that class was about to begin.

Renee put her purse down along the wall and lined up next to Joy, the connection there the strongest she'd had since moving to Brush Creek. "How long ago was that?" she asked.

"About ten years," she said. "What about you? Are you married?"

"Oh, no." Renee bent at the waist into a lunge position when everyone else did. Her back pulled like it hadn't been bent that way in a while. It hadn't. "I'm only twenty-four."

Joy laughed as she twisted from side to side, her midsection already toned and ready for whatever horrors lay ahead. "I was married and pregnant by twenty-four. Trust me, it can be done."

Renee paused in her stretching, marveling at the woman next to her. How did some people have everything so put together? When the instructor came toward her, she snapped back into motion, dismissing her thoughts. She was fine. She wasn't worth less because she was overweight, or because she wasn't married yet, or because she didn't put in garden spots.

"All right," the instructor called. The woman looked like she was made of steel and muscle. "Legs up, ladies!"

A groan escaped Renee's mouth when she saw how high the knees in the room went. She'd be lucky if she survived ten minutes of this class.

———

"OH, MY STARS," she said, her mouth already watering and they hadn't even gotten out of the truck yet. "It smells like syrup." She twisted back to Justin who draped one hand lazily over the steering wheel.

"You like syrup, obviously."

"Who doesn't like syrup?" She turned back to her open window, inhaling deeply the sweet, maple scent and letting it drift through her nose. She rationalized that she could eat the sugary syrup after that brutal workout. She'd left half her body weight in sweat on those black mats, seemingly the only woman in the room who dared to perspire.

Justin parked and Renee opened her door and slid from the truck, every muscle in her body protesting the movement.

"You okay?" Justin reached for her and slipped his arm around her back. "Why are you limping?"

She straightened her spine with great difficulty—and a groan. "I'm fine."

He eyed her suspiciously but let the topic drop. They moved through the line without incident, and Renee took one pancake when she normally would've taken two. With her phone at home and with light syrup on her single flapjack, Renee made it through breakfast with a smiling Justin. They walked over to Main Street from the park, where the parade would start in an hour.

"Landon always comes down on Friday night and saves a spot for the ranch," Justin explained on the short walk over. "I forgot to tell you that. Is it okay if we sit with them?"

Renee swung her hand waist-high, taking his with hers. "That's fine. I haven't met any of your friends."

"They're great," he said. "I think you'll like them." They crossed the street to the south side, where most of the trees stood. A section had been roped off with what looked like baling twine, and several camp chairs lined the grass where it met the sidewalk.

Renee recognized the family he'd come to the ice cream social with. Walker and Tess, if she remembered right. The two tween boys wrestled on a blanket in front of the row of chairs, and Renee couldn't remember their names.

Another tall cowboy with a set of twins stepped over the twine, a dark-haired woman with hair almost as curly as Renee's right behind him. She spread another blanket out and threw some toys onto it. The man set the toddlers on the ground and sat with them on the blanket while the woman settled into the chair behind them.

"Landon," Justin said, and the man with the twins glanced up. "This is Renee Martin."

Landon scrambled to his feet and grinned for all he was worth. "Renee, of course. You're the one who's been stealing Justin from us in the evenings."

Renee curled into Justin's side. "I've been trying."

Landon's smile felt infectious, and his eyes were in the same family of green as pine trees. "Well, come sit down." Landon gestured toward the chairs at the back of the space. "Do you know my wife, Megan?"

"No, I don't think we've met." Renee stepped over to the other woman, who welcomed her without a single shred of judgment in her dark eyes.

"I don't get off the ranch much," she confessed. "The twins keep me running from sunup to sundown."

"I bet." Renee settled into a chair with Justin next to her. He secured her hand in his again, almost like he didn't want to let her go. "So how many cowboys live up at the ranch?" she asked him.

He nodded at Walker and Landon. "Those two. Walker's the foreman. Landon's the owner of the ranch. There are four other cowboys. Ted, Grant, Emmett, and Blake." He glanced around like they'd all materialize out of thin air. "Blake's gone home for the weekend. His family lives in Colorado, only a few hours away. Grant has himself a new girl...somewhere, so he probably won't come. But Ted—"

"Has just arrived." A booming voice interrupted Justin and a bear of a man sank into the chair beside Justin's. "And this must be the beautiful woman you're always goin' on about during lunch."

Justin chuckled, but the sound got stuck in his throat. He glanced at Renee, and she adored the flush creeping up his throat. "Ted," he said. "This is Renee Martin."

Ted leaned forward, his black cowboy hat doing nothing to obscure his vibrant eyes the color of coal and his full beard. "Renee Martin, that's right. Nice to meet you." He extended his arm across Justin, who leaned back in his chair with a distasteful look on his face.

"Is Emmett coming?" Justin asked.

"He's parkin' the truck."

Several minutes later, another cowboy arrived, and Renee thought she'd mix them all up. They must've only sold one color of cowboy hat in town, because they all looked identical. No one ever took theirs off, though they must've been sweating underneath all that felt.

Renee didn't mind. Tess and Megan engaged her in conversation, and they didn't seem to mind that she was dating Justin. In fact, Tess said something along the lines of "it's about time he got serious about someone."

She'd laughed off the comment and when she'd glanced at Justin, he didn't seem to have heard as he was engaged in a conversation with Ted. While the band marched by, Renee stood and clapped along, a smile stuck to her face, but her mind racing.

Were she and Justin serious? They'd known each other for

a month. He hasn't dated in two years, she told herself. So yeah. Dating you for a month is probably pretty serious for him.

The smile became more genuine as her thoughts calmed and she accepted that maybe Justin liked her as much as she liked him.

CHAPTER 10

Weeks passed, and Justin settled into a familiar routine. He started rising a half an hour earlier so he could take Roy for a vigorous walk before it got too hot. He worked all day, ate lunch with the other boys, and went down to town in the evenings.

He liked spending time with Renee, but he certainly wasn't taking things to the next level. He'd heard what Tess had said at the parade, and it grated inside him every time he thought about it—which was every time he saw Tess or Walker, which was every stinking day.

He wasn't *serious* with Renee after only a couple of months. And even if he was, how would Tess know?

"Come on, boy," he called to his dog one morning in early August. The English shepherd poked his head up, his tongue hanging out of his mouth. A rush of affection for the dog dove through Justin. He loved Roy.

Just like he loved Renee.

He pushed the feelings away. So he'd developed a soft spot for the woman. Didn't mean he was in love with her.

But he did find himself looking at her the way he was currently watching Roy. With affection. With fondness for the simplest things.

Sometimes she'd fall asleep while they watched a movie, and he'd gaze down on her with that adoration curling through him. He found himself watching her when he showed up at her house and she was stirring something on the stove, her headphones in and dancing until she caught him leaning in the doorway, a satisfied smile on his face. The same smile he wore now as Roy tore through the sage brush with the ball in his mouth.

He dropped it at Justin's feet, who bent to retrieve it, scrubbing the dog's head affectionately. Justin sat on the ground and looked at the world around him. "What am I doing, Roy? Huh?"

The dog panted in response, put his front paws in Justin's lap, and collapsed next to him. He seemed to wear a perpetual smile, and Justin stole from the animal's calm demeanor.

"All right." He pushed himself to a standing position with a groan. "Time to get to work. C'mon." They walked back to the cabin, where Justin fed the dog and made sure he had plenty of cool water to drink. Then he headed across the lane to the ranch, where another fiery woman awaited him.

Red Star had settled a little over the course of the past couple of months, but she still had several hurdles to overcome before he could even bring out a rope. She'd been saddled, and he'd ridden her, but she needed to work on her focus and it would take months to get her to leap from the gate properly.

Justin didn't mind. Out here, he had nothing but time.

————

THAT NIGHT, just to prove he wasn't serious with Renee, he texted her to say he wouldn't be coming down to her bungalow.

Renee: Why not?

Justin: I'm tired. Been getting up early.

Renee: Maybe I can come up there.

Justin: If you want.

He never in a million years thought she'd come. But a couple of hours later, just as darkness was falling, someone knocked on his cabin door. It didn't sound like the burly knock of another cowboy—and they knocked and entered in the same breath anyway.

Justin launched himself off his couch, where he'd been dozing with Roy, and yanked open the door to find a sweaty, red-faced Renee standing on his porch. "Finally," she pushed past him and went straight into the kitchen.

He turned to watch her, more than a little stunned. "Did you walk up here?"

"I ran part of the way," she said over her shoulder as she filled a glass with water from his sink.

"Ran?" Justin practically whispered the word as he took in the curves of Renee's body in her tight workout clothes. He started toward her, suddenly realizing that his beautiful, curvy Renee was a little...bonier.

He slid his hand up her side as she drained the last of her water. He knew better than to ask a woman if she'd lost weight. He also had eyes, and while he hadn't noticed until now, looking down into Renee's face, he could definitely tell the lines of her face were more pronounced.

She stared up at him too, something akin to wonder in her expression. "What?" he asked.

"I don't think I've ever seen you without your cowboy hat." She reached up and ran her fingers lightly through his hair. "Yeah, this is nice." A smile bloomed on her face, and tingles flowed down Justin's back with the intimacy of her touch.

Unable to stop himself, he tipped his head down to kiss her. Her fingers along the back of his neck and in his hair caused the single best sensation he'd had while kissing a woman, and he vowed never to wear his cowboy hat again.

He forced himself to pull away when he wanted to keep kissing Renee. "You're sexy when you're sweaty," he growled into her ear, which elicited a little laugh that was much better than the giggle she usually emitted.

She began to sway, and he went with her, this dancing to silent music sweet and peaceful.

"Justin?" she murmured.

"Yeah?" He kneaded her closer, held her tighter.

"Where do you see this going?"

His comfort fled, and his grip tightened even more. "What? You mean us?"

"Yeah, I mean us." She nestled her face into the crook of his neck and took a deep breath, which set his nerve endings on fire.

"I know how relationships end," he said, gazing into the dusky sky outside his kitchen window. "There's only one of two ways, right?"

"A break-up or a wedding," she whispered.

He nodded, his mind churning. He didn't want to break up with Renee, that was for sure. But at the same time, he absolutely wasn't ready to marry her either.

His gut twisted. He wasn't even sure he could propose to a third woman for a third time. Intellectually, he knew the words to use. But getting his voice to say them?

Wasn't gonna happen.

She put a knuckle of distance between them, enough to lean back and look into his face. He appreciated the maturity he found there, wished he could erase the fear, basked in the affection.

"I think I'm in love with you," she whispered, the fear blanking from her eyes, leaving only the adoration, the passion.

Justin knew he should say it back. Tell her how he really felt.

But fear took hold of his vocal chords and squeezed, and he couldn't say anything.

———

A WEEK LATER, Justin muscled a bale of hay off the trailer and into the barn. He'd been working non-stop for days. That way he didn't have to think, didn't have to remember the way he'd just stood in his kitchen, mute. Didn't have to see the horror on Renee's beautiful face, didn't have to endure the silent ten-minute drive back to her house.

He'd tried to explain once he'd pulled into her driveway, but she held up one hand and said, "Don't, Justin." Her bottom lip wobbled, and her eyes filled with tears. "Call me later."

It was later, and he hadn't called. He expected she would, as Renee didn't keep anything bottled up for longer than five minutes. But she hadn't either, which testified of her extraordinary determination.

That, or she'd found someone else to talk to in the evenings.

Justin lifted a hay bale with each hand, hefting the fifty-pound weights and tossing them off the trailer. It was a bit too much weight for him, but it effectively erased Renee from his mind.

He tossed another bale and glanced up when a woman said, "Whoa. You almost hit me with that."

"Sorry, Megan." He straightened and pressed a kink from his back. "Is it time for lunch?"

"Lunch was two hours ago."

Justin frowned and tried to check his watch, but the leather gloves he wore prevented him from seeing the time. "Really?"

"I yelled at you from the backyard. You even waved, but you didn't come in."

"I'm sorry," he said, and he meant it. He glanced at the half-full trailer of hay bales. "Must've just gotten busy."

"I've never known your stomach to miss a meal." She cocked her head and peered at him. "I haven't seen you leaving the ranch in the evenings the way you used to."

"Been busy." He jumped down from the trailer, eager to wrap up this conversation. "I'll go grab something at home. Sorry I missed lunch."

"No problem."

He walked away, but he felt the weight of her eyes on

his back. He wondered what she'd tell Landon, and if he'd show up on Justin's doorstep to lecture him about love.

It took another week, and Landon didn't come alone. Walker stood with him, and Megan had clearly spent most of the afternoon in the kitchen, because Landon carried a paper plate full of chocolate chip cookies.

His biggest weakness, blast them all.

"I guess you better come in." He stepped back from the door. "Hottest week of the summer, and you're lettin' all the air conditioning out."

Walker cocked one eyebrow. "Are you an eighty-year-old woman now?" He chuckled as he entered the house. "But it does feel good in here."

Landon followed Justin into the kitchen and unwrapped the plate of cookies. "Megan is worried about you."

"Why? I'm just fine."

"You've reverted back to how you were when you first came to us."

"I was fine then too."

Walker scoffed as he picked up a cookie. "Yeah, you were happy and full of life. Walkin' your dog in the mornings, going fishing every weekend, whistling while you worked for those first few months. Then you dressed yourself up real nice and went down to the church. You came back a different man, JayJ."

Justin sighed and grabbed a couple of cookies, but the thought of actually putting one in his mouth made him twitchy.

"You're turning back into him," Walker said. "And I don't like it."

"You were happy with Renee," Landon said. "What happened?"

Justin took his cookies into the living room and collapsed onto the couch. "She told me she was in love with me." He didn't have to look at his friends to know they'd exchanged a glance. "And I just...can't deal with that right now."

"You don't want a pretty woman in your life?" Walker leaned against the wall near the door and put almost a whole cookie in his mouth.

Justin knew his friends wouldn't understand. He couldn't expect them to; never had. They hadn't endured two failed engagements.

"I just couldn't get myself to say it," he said. "I just—I can't—I don't think I'm quite ready to be at that level, and I may have panicked."

Walker's brow creased, and Justin didn't like the look on the foreman's face. "Maybe you shouldn't have started dating her if you weren't ready."

Anger and humiliation made his insides thrash. "I wasn't expecting to feel so strongly about Renee so quickly."

"Millennials do everything quickly," Landon said. "Heck, I wouldn't be surprised if she's already found another boyfriend."

The very idea made Justin see green as pure jealousy coated every cell. "No." He shook his head.

"Maybe you should call her and find out." Landon knocked on the counter and headed for the front door. Walker went with him, the intervention over.

Relief made Justin's muscles sag, and he took a bite of

his cookie, beyond confused about what to do. He swallowed and tipped his head back, his eyes tracing lines on the ceiling as he prayed more fervently than he ever had before.

Before he finished, he already knew what he had to do.

Swallow your pride.

Justin tried to complete the action physically, and it made his throat hurt. He had no idea how to swallow his pride, because it seemed too big to even approach in small bites.

Chapter 11

"Yes, yes," Renee said into the phone as she tossed her toothbrush into an overnight bag. "I'll be there in the morning."

Her boss wanted her in Moab by morning, and as it was already nearing seven p.m., the four-hour drive would have her arriving late enough to make her cranky.

She hung up and muttered, "Couldn't he have let me know sooner?"

But she'd learned that sometimes memos in the National Parks Department got lost, misplaced, or down-right deleted.

But her boss had assured her that he was very pleased with her work in getting more traffic out to Dinosaur as they'd seen a seven percent increase in visitors since she'd started as the social media coordinator.

She finished packing and opened the fridge, like she'd have anything good to eat inside. She didn't, of course. She hadn't for a couple of months now, and she could really use a vat of ice cream about now.

The last time she'd talked to Justin flashed through her mind. The morning after he'd dropped her off, she'd waited around for hours, just knowing he was going to call. When he hadn't, she'd bought every flavor of ice cream the grocer carried. And then she'd gotten right back on her diet. She was down seventeen pounds, thank you very much, but she no longer had a reason to starve herself.

Deciding to get Chinese takeout as she passed through Vernal, she snatched her keys from the kitchen table, shouldered her purse, and retrieved the suitcase from her bedroom.

She pulled open the front door and nearly smashed into Justin, who stood on the porch, one hand falling to his side as if he were about to knock.

She sucked in a breath, her heartbeat vibrating through her whole body like bass turned up too loud. She couldn't even form his name; she just stared at him. He wore that sexy cowboy hat, a red short-sleeved shirt, and his jeans. She'd seen him in an outfit similar to this on many occasions. Opened her front door to find him waiting for her on the other side for dozens of evenings in a row. Somehow, now, the sight of him made her numb, cold.

"You leaving town?" he asked.

Everything that had frozen at the glorious sight of him thawed. "Yes," she said. "I have a business meeting in the morning in Moab."

He shoved his hands in his pockets. "So I guess now isn't a good time to talk."

She stepped out of the house, forcing him to back up, and locked the door after she pulled it closed. "It's not. Sorry."

Three weeks. The man had left her in silence for three full weeks. They'd missed the apricot festival. Renee hadn't been able to force herself to go, even when Leah called and begged. She hadn't tasted a single bite of the town's famous apricot preserves, and she'd probably read twenty books in the past three weeks.

Seeing him standing there, all gorgeous and humble, set fire to her blood, and not in a good way. She stepped away from him, half-hoping he'd call her back, beg her to talk to him.

"So I'll call you tomorrow," he said.

She laughed, the bitter notes of it clear and loud in the autumn evening. "Right. I won't hold my breath." She unlocked her car and popped the trunk. She started to lift her suitcase, and then Justin was there, effortlessly taking it from her and depositing it in the trunk.

"I *will* call tomorrow." His gaze burned into hers.

"I don't know what my schedule is like." She wanted to melt into him, kiss him good-bye, thank him for finally coming around. At the same time, she deserved a proper explanation for his sudden loss of speech three weeks ago, for his radio silence, after she'd told him she loved him.

"Look, I owe you an explanation." He closed the trunk. "Will you be home tomorrow night? Maybe we can go to dinner."

Helplessness filled her. "I don't know. My boss didn't detail why he needed me in Moab." She lifted her chin. "But when I get back in town, I think dinner sounds like a good idea."

Half a smile formed on his face. "All right, then."

She pushed him in the chest. "Don't be so proud of yourself, Mister. You have a long way to go."

His boots scuffed the ground. "I'm not proud," he said. "At least I'm trying not to be."

She studied him and found the remorse in his eyes. "I'll text you when I'm done with my meetings."

His face lit up and she basked in the warmth of it before ducking into her car.

———

BY NOON THE NEXT DAY, Renee was ready to shed her fancy-schmancy business skirt—which she'd purchased specifically to meet her boss for the first time face-to-face, *and* which was two sizes smaller than she normally wore—and text Justin to jump in his truck and take her to dinner in Moab.

Because Steve never—stopped—talking. Though the man had twenty years on her, he was a gabber, and Renee couldn't wait to get out of the conference room. She and two other social media coordinators had been suffering for the past four hours, and Steven hadn't said much of anything.

Renee had given a presentation on her use of hashtags, and how she'd been using pithy comments about dinosaurs, including using the specific types of them, to get more eyes on her tweets, her Facebook ads, and their instagram pictures. That had been a fun discussion, but it had lasted twenty minutes and she hadn't prepared anything, because Steven hadn't asked her to.

Luckily, she knew enough and had enough experience with all things social media that she could talk about them in her sleep. In fact, she probably did.

By three o'clock, she knew she wouldn't make it back to Brush Creek in time for dinner that night. On a weekday, nothing stayed open past eight, and even if she drove as fast as her sedan would allow her, they'd have less than an hour for dinner.

She excused herself and stepped into the sunshine to text Justin.

Renee: Not gonna make it to dinner tonight. Sorry.

Justin, only seconds later: Still in meetings?

Renee: All day long. I want to die.

Justin: Not much of a meeting guy myself.

Renee: No kidding? I had no idea. ;)

Justin: Ha ha. What did your boss want to tell you?

Renee: He likes my work. I gave a presentation and everything. Not really using my resource management degree, but I like tweeting.

Justin: I'm not even sure how to tweet.

Renee: Whatever. I looked you up. JJ Roping Man, if I remember right.

Justin: I have never tweeted. My manager did that.

Renee: Ohhh, your big shot manager. I see how it is.

Justin: I used to be a professional in the rodeo.

Renee: Another mystery solved. Also, can I start calling you JJ?

Justin: In your dreams.

Renee: Oh, I have dreams about you.

Justin: We can talk about those at dinner too.

Renee: I should be done here in a couple of hours. Call me about 7:00?

Justin: Deal.

Renee pressed her phone to her chest, trying—and failing—not to forgive Justin so fast. But she couldn't help it. Just like she couldn't keep the bet a secret the first time they'd talked, she couldn't reason away her feelings. Sure, some of them were hurt, but just talking to Justin again soothed the wounds.

Her phone rang, startling her. It wasn't Justin, but her mom. "Hey, Mom. What's up?"

"Just calling to check in."

"It's not a great time. I'm supposed to be in a meeting."

"Oh, is this the Moab thing you texted me about?"

"Yes, and I just stepped out to text Justin."

A healthy pause on the other end of the line revealed why her mom had really called. Renee didn't mind. She liked talking to her mom, and she'd been calling a lot more often since Justin had gone silent. So what if the first time she'd been crying?

"So you're talking to him again?"

"He showed up on my doorstep last night."

"And?"

"And nothing. I was leaving town. We barely spoke, and I just texted him about the awful meetings."

Steve appeared on the other side of the window, clearly looking for her. She held up one finger to indicate she'd be another moment. A moment of frustration stole across his face and then he lifted his hand to indicate she should take her time before he turned and left.

"How do you feel about him?"

Renee sighed. "My boss is looking for me, and that question is impossible to answer anyway."

"It shouldn't be."

"It's going to take some time," Renee said. "My heart is cracked."

"But it's not broken," her mom singsonged.

Renee couldn't help smiling. No, her heart wasn't completely broken, and she knew a very handy cowboy that would have her fixed up in no time—if he could find the right words to say.

She hung up with her mother and took a few more moments in the sunshine. She did love Justin Jackman, she was sure of it. She'd prayed over the last three weeks to know for sure, and God had given her the answer. Justin was "the one" for her. She had then started praying that she'd be the one for him, but the Lord had been less than forthcoming on that.

She tilted her head heavenward and offered her latest rendition of a prayer. "If it be Thy will, please bring him back to me." Nothing more. She was tired of trying to be the perfect woman for him. He certainly wasn't a perfect man. But he was hardworking, and caring, and kind, and everything she'd hoped to have in a husband.

She had dreamt of him, of what life would be like in that cowboy cabin of his at the top of the canyon. And she'd been happy in the dreams, with all the babies she'd always fantasized about having. Maybe she could keep designing social media campaigns for the Parks Department too. She didn't know.

What she did know was that she was needed back in the

meeting. She knew God loved her. And she knew that if she simply kept putting one foot in front of the other, that someday, she'd find her happily-ever-after.

She could only hope—and keep praying—that it was with Justin.

CHAPTER 12

Justin endured a couple of restless days, knowing Renee wasn't just a quick nine-minute drive down the canyon. At the same time, now that they were talking again, a measure of relief had infused his life. Relief that he'd been living without for too long.

Friday after work, he entered his cabin and scrubbed the top of his dog's head. "Hey, boy." At least he wasn't completely alone. His footsteps faltered as he realized he didn't want to be alone for the rest of his life. And a dog for company wasn't nearly enough when compared to Renee.

Help me tell her I love her, he prayed as he stepped into the shower. She'd texted a couple of hours ago to say she'd just left Moab. He'd be early, but he didn't care. He wanted to see her the moment she stepped from her car, wrap her in his arms, and whisper the three words she needed to hear.

An urgency to get to her house coursed through him, and he lathered up faster. He arrived at her house and parked on the street so she could pull into her driveway when she got there. She'd replaced the metal, rusted table and chairs on her front porch with a flirtier, fun version that fit her personality.

He settled into one of the white wicker chairs, glad for the teal and white striped cushion she'd put on it. Teal and yellow wicker pieces adorned the table legs, and Justin ran his finger along one as a slight breeze touched the brim of his cowboy hat.

"Renee," he said out loud, glad the neighboring houses weren't too close. "I—I." He exhaled in frustration. He'd been the first to tell both Paulette and Tina, the women he'd proposed to, that he loved them. He remembered the rush of saying those words, the excitement when they were repeated back to him.

He rubbed his palm over his clean-shaven face. He couldn't believe he hadn't responded when Renee had first told him she loved him.

I love you, Renee, he thought, but his throat seized.

"I—love—you." The words scraped his throat and he wished he'd brought a bottle of water with him. By the time Renee arrived, he wouldn't be able to say hello, much less I love you.

"You have to tell her," he said, a thread of agony pulling through him. He didn't want to lose her, and she'd spoken true that relationships only ended in one of two ways: a break-up or a wedding.

His phone rang, and his heart jumped to the back of his throat. But it was only his brother. Justin considered sending the call to voice mail, but his brother rarely called, so he answered.

"JayJ," Harvey said, his voice jovial and too loud. Harvey had a tendency to yell everything he said. Justin had always looked up to his older brother, and it had been a while since he'd spoken with him.

"Hey, Harve. What's up?" He scanned the street, but all he saw was a couple of children running with a dog in a yard a few houses down. He knew from Walker that school started on Tuesday, and this was the last weekend of freedom for the kids.

"I'm hosting Thanksgiving dinner at my house this year," Harvey said. "I wanted to call and personally invite you."

"Mom put you up to this, didn't she?" Justin sounded accusatory, but a smile graced his face. "Because I haven't been home in a couple of years."

"Alex wants everyone together," he said, referencing his wife. "Since we moved into our new house, she's been dying to have the whole family here."

Justin thought about the sunny skies in California, the sandy beaches, the way he seriously needed a vacation. "You'll put a baby gate up for me, right?" he asked with a chuckle. "Mom says your house is like six levels."

Harvey laughed, and Justin pulled the phone from his ear lest he go deaf. "It's not six levels. Okay, there are a lot of little levels, like three or four stairs. I'm sure Alex has a baby gate in the garage or something." He laughed again, quieter this time. "Does this mean you'll come?"

"Yeah." Justin exhaled. "Plan on me. And...can I bring my girlfriend?"

"Shut the front door." Harvey whooped. "What's her name? How serious is it? Have you told Mom? Of course you haven't told her, because she would've mentioned it to me. Wow, JayJ. Just wow."

Justin looked up to the sky and didn't even try to contain the grin or the happiness. "Her name is Renee, and —" A car came around the corner. "She just got here. I have to go." He hung up amidst a very loud protest from his brother. He gripped the phone tight, tight, and then placed it on the table beside him. He tossed back half a container of orange Tic Tacs and moved to the top of the steps, where he leaned against the pillar, containing his hands in his pockets so she wouldn't be able to see the tension in his fists.

She pulled into the driveway and took her sweet time gathering her purse, a water bottle, and her phone before emerging from the sedan. "Hey, there," she called, smoothing down her blouse in what Justin recognized as one of her nervous gestures. She wore a business jacket and skirt, with a pale pink blouse underneath—clothes he'd never seen her in. She was so sexy his breath caught in his throat and he couldn't tear his eyes from her.

He swallowed hard as she approached, barely able to keep himself from rushing down the stairs and taking her in his arms—where she fit.

"Hey, yourself," he finally managed to say. "How was Moab?"

She sighed as she fumbled for her keys in her purse, her eyes averted from his as she stepped past him. Disappointment cut hard through his gut, making it even harder to swallow.

"It made me more grateful for my work-from-home job." She flashed him a brief smile and stuck the key in her front door.

She'd only been gone for two days, but her house

smelled a bit stale. Justin shut the door behind him, sealing them in navy darkness until Renee flipped on some lights. She disappeared around the corner, leaving Justin to wonder where he should wait.

When she didn't return in only a few seconds, he sank onto her couch. Renee came out ten minutes later wearing her more familiar jeans and a cotton T-shirt. He waited for her to look at him, but she didn't. She started a pot of coffee without speaking and bustled around the kitchen while humming softly in her throat.

Justin couldn't take another moment of this awkward vibe between them. "I thought we were goin' to dinner." He stood, his insides buzzing like someone had hooked him up to a live electrical line.

"I'm tired." She pulled a loaf of bread out of the freezer. "Do you mind if we stay in?"

He joined her in the kitchen and put his hand on her arm, which caused her to freeze. "Renee," he said, his voice barely louder than silence.

She turned toward him, and all his carefully ordered words, his apologies, all his explanations, flew out of his mind. He leaned closer, drew in a deep breath of her soft, fresh scent, and whispered, "It's so good to see you."

Her eyes locked onto his, and he let himself fall right into the dazzling depths of her hazel gaze. "Don't pretend like you don't want to hear everything I have to say," he said now that he finally had her full attention. A smile kicked itself across his mouth, and he brought his hands up to cradle her face.

"I'll start with the most important thing." His heart

thundered in his chest, the storm he'd been holding in for three weeks ready to be released.

"Renee, I love you."

She blinked, the disbelief in her eyes leaking away when he said, "I'm in love with you, and I'll tell you everyday of your life until—"

"All right," she said, her hands finally coming around him, finally leaning into him. "Can you kiss me now?"

Justin touched his lips to her forehead. "I love you, Renee."

She moaned. "Wrong spot."

"Oh yeah?" He smiled down at her. "Where would you like me to kiss you?" He pressed his mouth against her cheekbone. "Here?"

"You're mean," she whispered, one of her hands taking the back of his cowboy hat and pulling it off.

"But you love me anyway." He trailed his lips along her jaw to her ear.

She trembled in his arms. "I do love you anyway."

He took an extra heartbeat to gaze at her, another moment to say, "I love you," one more time before finally uniting his mouth with hers.

CHAPTER 13

Renee had never been kissed by a man who loved her. It felt wonderful, a curling sensation that wafted through her body like smoke. She could feel his love in the touch, the careful way he explored her mouth, the tightness with which he held her body next to his.

She never wanted Justin to stop. Always wanted to be with him. Craved the taste of those orange mints he carried everywhere with him. Needed the opportunity to build a life with him.

For the entire four-hour drive home she'd coached herself to make him work for her forgiveness. Well, she'd talked everything through with her mom for the first hour, but still. Now that the moment was here, though, she realized she'd already forgiven him. He'd tell her everything anyway, she knew, but for now, she just wanted to keep kissing him.

He finally pulled away, his pulse pounding under her fingertips. He chuckled, laced his fingers through hers and led her to the couch. He tucked her into his side, and she liked the strength and power of him next to her.

Renee closed her eyes and sent a prayer of thanksgiving to the Lord. Thank you for bringing him home to me. Thank you for putting me here in Brush Creek.

She hadn't thought she'd be here for longer than a few weeks, but God worked in mysterious ways, led her down roads she hadn't been able to see.

"Steve—that's my boss—wants me to take a regional job."

"Oh yeah?" He threaded his fingers through her hair. "What does that mean?"

"He wants me to take over the online campaigns for Arches and Canyonlands National Parks, in addition to what I'm still doing with Dinosaur."

His fingers trailed up and down her bare arm, which sent cascades of delight through her. "Sounds like you'll be three times as busy then."

"Just at first, while I learn the particulars of the parks." She pushed one palm against his chest. "And now's your big chance. I need to visit the parks, do the hikes, take some notes on what makes them unique, what will get more people inside." She tipped up and pressed a quick kiss to his mouth. "Will you take me hiking at Arches?"

"Hmm." He gazed down at her with pure love in his expression. "Can we go fishing too?"

She flinched, but said, "Sure," with a hard swallow.

Justin laughed and tucked her back into his side. "So I have a favor too. Maybe we can make a deal."

"This better not involve a bet and a hot dog cart." They laughed together, and Renee wondered if this could really be her adult life. A job she liked and was good at. A man who made her pulse thrum just by coming closer. Wit, and orange Tic Tacs, and fishing on the weekends. Well, she might be able to do without the fishing. She wasn't sure, as she'd actually never been fishing before.

"There might be some hot dogs, actually. My brother lives in California, and he's always bragging about his outdoor kitchen, equipped with the biggest gas grill a man can buy."

"Okay," she said slowly, not quite on the same page as him yet.

"He called and invited me for Thanksgiving dinner. I told him I'd come. I'm hoping you'll want to come with me."

She snuggled in closer to him, enjoying the warmth from his body. "Of course I want to go with you. California in November sounds wonderful."

"Oh, so you're using me to get a vacation to the beach in the winter." He chuckled, the sound grumbly and echoing through his chest, where her ear was pressed. "My whole family will be there. It'll be nuts."

"You don't know the meaning of nuts," she said. "Remember how I have nine siblings? Simply getting up and going to school was a national event."

"So we'll go hiking and fishing at the National Parks, and then we'll go to Long Beach for Thanksgiving."

"This is the best deal I've ever made."

———

"I CANNOT IMAGINE anyone wanting to do this," Renee complained as she faced yet another steep incline. Sure, the red rocks at Arches were unlike any she'd ever seen before. The way the wind and water carved stone into arches was breathtaking.

But the heat. Holy stars, the heat. And it was the middle of September, not the middle of summer. How in the world was she going to entice visitors to come to the parks in mid-July?

She snapped photos of the magnificent double-arch, deciding to leave out the part where she had to hike half a mile in loose, red sand to get there. The cavern the arches created made for a perfect lunch and resting spot, as evidenced by the people strung out along the rocks. She sighed with relief. Eating had been the best part of this week-long excursion through Canyonlands and Arches.

Tomorrow, they had one more hike to complete—the hardest one, which led up to one of the most visited sites in Utah: Delicate Arch.

She'd enjoyed her week with Justin; she felt pampered from the attention he lavished on her; something nagged at her. She didn't want to go to California in a couple of months without wearing a wedding ring. But after talking everything through with Justin, she knew he wouldn't propose before Thanksgiving.

"It's not that I don't want to," he'd said. "It's just that... I can't right now." His blue eyes had blazed with pure emotion, pure desperation, when he'd added, "I hope you understand."

She didn't, not really. But she'd never been engaged at all, let alone twice. And when he'd admitted that Paulette had stood him up on their wedding day, Renee had stuffed her need for an engagement ring to the bottom of her shoes. It sat there like a pebble, rubbing her feet the wrong way whenever she paid too much attention to it.

She'd said she didn't need a diamond to be with him. She'd kissed him like she meant it, because in that moment, she had. They'd been dating for three months, and she could be patient until he was ready to take their relationship to the diamond level.

"Turkey and Swiss for you," Justin said, drawing a zipper bag with a sandwich inside out of his backpack. "And your Tic Tacs." He tossed a container of the orange treats to the ground. "Make sure you eat all of those before kissin' me," he said. "I really don't like Swiss cheese." The playful grin he gave her made her giggle.

"Who says we'll be kissing at all?"

"Your phone. You're not gonna use any of our pictures online, right?"

"Of course not," she said for at least the hundredth time. She'd been taking selfies of them at every arch they'd come to, most of them with her kissing him on the cheek or mouth. She looked at them in her hotel room, reliving some of the best days of her life, even if she didn't enjoy hiking on a fundamental level.

"There's no hiking in California, right?" She bit into her sandwich, but not even mayo and turkey on white bread could soothe her sore feet.

"Just walking down the beach." He leaned over and pressed a kiss to her temple.

Renee eyed the red sand below with distaste, cursing it

for ruining her fantasies of walking on the beach, hand-in-hand with Justin.

———

THE MONTHS PASSED QUICKLY for Renee. It took her a solid six weeks to figure out a marketing strategy for the three sites she'd be managing. She drove to Moab every other week and skipped Halloween due to her loathing of the holiday. Justin didn't like the holiday either, much to her relief.

When the weather was good, she walked and ran the three miles up to Justin's cabin in the evenings. He always rewarded her with a bone-melting kiss and a bowl full of ice cream. As fall descended on the mountain town, so did rain and snow. On those days, Justin drove down the canyon and sipped coffee, hot chocolate, or wassail on Renee's couch with her curled into his side.

She'd learned that he wanted kids but didn't have an opinion on how many. He'd told her that the Internet at the ranch was top-notch. All of their conversations danced around the fact that they were planning their lives together.

And yet, no proposal had come.

Renee sighed as she laid her flip flops on top of the rest of her clothes. "Toiletries in the morning," she muttered to herself. Justin was picking her up early and their flight to Long Beach would have them arriving by mid-afternoon. Renee could practically feel the sun's rays on her face right now.

"Hello?" Justin's voice carried down the hall from the front door. "I'm coming in. It's freezing out here."

She gained the corner just as he shut the snow and wind out. He brushed off his coat and shivered. "Storm's bad. Hope we can make it to Salt Lake tomorrow."

"I read on the Internet that the storm will pass by morning. The ploughs will have the main roads clear." She smiled at him. "I hope you're hungry, because Joy came over today, and she seemed to think I needed three loaves of bread before I left town for a week."

He swept into her personal space and embraced her. "Did you tell her you don't eat bread?"

"I eat bread sometimes." She held onto his strong biceps. "Especially when I make soup."

He looked over her head toward the kitchen. "What kind of soup?"

"Loaded baked potato."

He groaned and released her. "I knew I could smell bacon."

She pointed to the two paper bags sitting on the table. "Can you take those up to the other boys? We'll have one for dinner."

"Sure. Ted's a carb fanatic."

"A kindred spirit." She'd stuck to her diet, though she cheated from time to time. She hadn't lost much more weight—maybe ten more pounds—and she still carried extra baggage in her midsection. But she was happy where she was.

As she lifted the lid and stirred the soup, her gaze landed on her left hand. Her naked ring finger seemed to mock her, and she realized there was one thing that would make her a tad happier.

———

"WE'RE HERE." Renee couldn't wait to get to the beach. The Long Beach Airport was the best thing she'd seen in a long time, and the ocean breeze tickling her face made her eyes drift closed in bliss. "Justin, we're here."

"I'm aware." He glanced right and left. "Car rentals over there." They got the car and Renee rolled down her window to enjoy the California air as much as possible on the way to Justin's brother's house.

"So his wife's name is Alex," Justin told her again. "He's Harvey. And he has three girls, Lauren, Amanda, and Halle, like the actress."

"Right," Renee said. "And your other brother won't be here until tomorrow?"

"Yeah, he's coming in with my parents. They all still live in Kentucky."

Renee nodded, her gut still churning. She wasn't sure why, other than she hadn't had much practice meeting her boyfriend's family. Zero practice, in fact. Justin pulled into a driveway in front of a large home in a nice neighborhood and killed the engine.

"I'll get the luggage." He got out of the car and stretched his long legs. Renee followed him, taking only her purse as she bathed in the warmth. It wasn't fair that California enjoyed such nice weather when Utah was buried in snow.

The front door burst open and three girls with dark hair and olive skin spilled out. "Uncle Justin!" the littlest one called, and Justin abandoned the luggage in favor of scooping up all three girls at once.

They squealed and laughed. His hat hit the pavement. Renee stooped to pick it up, admiring the way he clearly adored his nieces, even if he hadn't seen them in a couple of years.

"Ladies," he said, stepping back. "This is my girlfriend, Renee." He reached for his hat and mashed it back on his head before slipping his fingers into hers.

She met Lauren, an eleven-year old, Amanda, who was nine, and Halle, who was only five. "Did you start kinder-garten this year?" Renee asked her, crouching down to be at the girl's height.

That set the girl talking, and Justin herded everyone toward the house, where a Hispanic woman stood in the doorway, a smile on her face. She embraced Justin too and said something in his ear before he continued into the house.

She cast fond looks to each of her daughters as they passed, adding, "Get out the treats we made for our guests, all right?" When she turned back to Renee, the same acceptance and happiness that Renee had seen on Joy's face the first time they met passed across Alex's expression.

"And you must be Renee." She drew Renee into a hug. "Welcome. You must be someone special to break Justin's female-free diet."

Renee smiled at her. "Oh, I'm not special. I only met him because of a bet."

"At a bar," Justin added as he returned. "Don't leave that part out."

Renee rolled her eyes. "We were *not* at a bar."

"I should hope not." A male voice that had notes of familiarity sounded behind Renee, and she turned toward an image of Justin. There were obvious differences in the nose and chin, as well as the fact that Harvey weighed at least fifty pounds more than his brother. Everything about him was rounder, where Justin was lean and strong.

"Your brother is a pastor." Renee swung her attention back to Justin.

"You haven't told her about me?" Harvey spoke in a hurt tone, but the grin on his face gave him away. He stepped past Renee and engulfed his younger brother in a crushing hug. They laughed and Renee wanted to bottle it and hear it everyday for the rest of her life.

"So," Harvey said. "This is Renee." Before she could move, he'd grabbed her too and lifted her right off her feet as he hugged her.

"All right, Harve. Enough." Justin chuckled as Harvey set Renee down. She gave a nervous laugh as she straightened her clothes.

"So, who's hungry?" Alex asked, turning toward the interior of the house. Everyone followed her, and Renee stopped worrying about what she'd eat. The kitchen counter bore trays and platters of all shapes and sizes, with vegetables and dip, chips and salsa, small sausages in some sort of sauce, cookies, crackers, and rice crispy treats. Renee plucked one of those from the tray and took a big bite.

The sugar and butter calmed her upon contact. She sighed and looked out the sliding glass door—and choked. "You have a pool?" She volleyed her gaze from Alex to Justin to Harvey.

"It's not heated," Harvey said. "It'll be cold, but you can get in if you want."

"No." Renee shook her head. "No, I don't want to get

in. I just want to sit by it." She took one step and then paused. "Can I? Just go sit by it?"

"It's snowing in Utah," Justin said by way of explanation, and Alex gestured for Renee to step out onto the back patio.

"I'll bring you a drink," Alex said. She brought a diet cola—Renee's favorite—and sat by her in the lounger.

"It's so warm here," Renee said, popping the top on her soda. "You have a lovely home. Cute daughters. Thanks for having us."

"Anytime. We'd love more visitors."

Renee smiled and leaned her head back against the lounge chair, the sun painting her vision in golds and whites. "We'll probably need to get married before we come again. That'll be a while though."

"Oh?" The interest in Alex's voice could've called dogs. "What do you mean?"

Renee's eyes snapped open, and she was momentarily blinded. "I—I just—"

"You want him to propose and he won't." She started nodding at the hedges across the pool.

"No, I just—" Renee hung her head. "We talk all the time about our future. How many kids we want. If we'll live up at the ranch or in the valley. But he hasn't once brought up going ring shopping or setting a date." She held up her hand when Alex opened her mouth. "I mean, I get it. Paulette really destroyed him."

Alex cocked her head, and Renee didn't like the intense edge in her eyes. "How old are you, Renee?"

"Twenty-four."

"A true millennial."

"I guess."

"Justin said you work online."

"I'm a regional social media coordinator."

Alex tipped her head back and laughed, her dark-as-night hair trailing across her shoulders. "Definitely a millennial."

"What does that have to do with anything?"

She leaned closer, a spark of friendship leaping in her eyes. "You want to get engaged? Ask him to marry you." She sat back, her message delivered.

Shock sang through Renee. "I don't know.... Would he be okay with that?"

"I've known Justin since he was eighteen years old," she said. "He's been burned badly twice. He probably wants to get engaged, but he can't get himself there mentally. But you're already there. So *you* do it." With that, she laid back and closed her eyes.

Renee copied her, but the earlier peace and tranquility didn't come.

CHAPTER 14

On Thanksgiving Day, Justin ate a lot of turkey and pecan pie. He bypassed the pumpkin, much to Renee's consternation.

"I can't believe you don't like pumpkin pie!" she'd cried, her eyes wide. "That's it. Give me his piece." And she'd eaten them both too. Charmed his parents with her infectious laugh and played with his nieces and nephews like they were her own.

"She's wonderful," his mom whispered to him while Renee went into the kitchen to refill her coffee mug.

"Mom," he hissed. "Not now."

But she wouldn't be deterred. With one eye still on Renee, who laughed with Alex in the kitchen, his mom asked, "Are you going to ask her to marry you?"

Justin had thought of little else since she'd come to his cabin after a business trip a few weeks ago. She'd declared his loft as "the perfect workspace" for her at-home work. She'd asked about the Internet, and he'd told her the ranch had excellent service. It was as if they were making plans to live together very soon.

Which meant they'd be getting married very soon.

He'd had almost a month, and he still hadn't been able to pluck up the courage to ask her. He'd done it twice to other women; he knew the words to say.

Renee returned before Justin could answer his mom. She exuded joy as she sank onto the couch next to him. "Hey, you wanna get out of here for a while?" He'd had enough of the crowd and wanted to talk to Renee alone.

"Is that a possibility?" she asked, casting a glance at his parents. Thankfully, his mom had gone back to her conversation with his dad and Jeff, his other brother.

"Yes." He stood and took her coffee cup. "Renee and I are going to the beach."

All conversation stopped, and Justin glanced around at his family, glad he'd made this trip. It really had been too long since he'd seen them. "Who wants to go?"

Everyone wanted to go, of course. So bags got packed and cars loaded, and Harvey led a caravan of vehicles to the beach. There weren't very many people there, and Justin was easily able to separate Renee from everyone else.

"So, what do you think?" he asked as his toes sank into the sand. He wore shorts, a real rarity for him, and he wandered a bit closer to the shore.

"Of your family?"

"Yeah, my parents got in late last night, and you didn't really get to talk to them. And Jeff's...well, Jeff's a little on the odd side."

"I thought he was nice." She stepped into the surf and

smiled. "I really like them all. We'll have to meet my family in batches so you don't go crazy."

"When do you think that will happen?"

"We could go meet my parents anytime. They're in Idaho Falls. I have five older siblings, and they're sort of all over the west and Midwest. The twins are at college in Boise. And there are still two kids at home."

Justin's head spun just keeping track of all of that, and she hadn't even told him any of their names—besides Julia, who she'd texted during the concert in the park.

"What's Christmas like in Idaho Falls?"

She cast him a quick glance out of the corner of her eye. "I'll have to call my mom and ask her who's coming home this year. My guess is it will be an eleven on an insanity scale of one to ten."

"Maybe it's time to get a little insane," he said, not quite sure where the words had come from or what they meant.

Renee laughed, the sound rising into the sky and floating away. "Right. You don't do insane."

"I could handle it."

"You aren't even handling your own family well, and you only have two brothers."

"There are seven kids between them."

"I have more siblings than that." She paused, pulling on him to stop walking too. "Justin, I don't care. I get that you come from a quiet cabin where you live with a dog that I've never heard bark."

"Roy is a great dog," he said, his voice defensive. "You said you liked him." Justin wasn't sure what he'd do if he had to give up his dog.

She grinned and draped herself in his arms. "Of course I

like him." She tipped up on her toes and pressed a kiss to his mouth. "And I love you, anti-social and anti-crowd as you are. I'm just saying we should meet my family in batches."

Switching her focus forward again, she tugged on his hand and got him moving again. "So I'll call my mom and find out about Christmas."

"Deal," he said, the sun glinting like diamonds on the ocean.

Diamonds, he thought. He wondered if he could give Renee a diamond before they went to Idaho for Christmas. His mouth turned dry and his heart hammered at the very thought, yet a smile also curled the corners of his mouth.

Maybe....

Two weeks later, he found Renee in his kitchen, a pot of coffee already brewed when he finished work. "Hey." He kissed her quickly because he smelled like horse and hay and worse. "This is a nice surprise." He scanned the counter, where a box from Luigi's sat. "And you brought dinner too. My birthday isn't until March, beautiful."

She smiled, but it contained a secret. Her eyes harbored one too. He studied her. "What's goin' on?"

"You go shower, and then we'll talk about it."

He complied, thinking whatever it was must not be too important, or she wouldn't send him to shower first. Still, he hurried through the motions and returned to her in the kitchen. He opened the box of pizza and tossed three slices onto a plate.

When Renee didn't even reach for a plate, he stalled. "Are we eating or talking first?"

She took his plate and set it on the counter. "Justin, I'm in love with you, and we've been talking about our future together." She opened his bread drawer and removed a navy blue ring box. Justin's heart shot straight out of his chest. At least it felt like it did, because he couldn't breathe, and he couldn't blink, and he couldn't speak.

"I found a ring that I really love, and I'm wondering if you'd like to marry me." She cracked open the ring box and tilted it toward him, but he didn't even look at it.

She laughed but it came off more as a cackle. "I'm probably doing this all wrong. It's my first proposal."

"You're doing fine," he said. He spun away from her. "Renee, this—"

"I know this isn't traditional," she said. "But I'm a millennial. We don't do traditional." She stepped around him and faced him again. "So will you marry me?"

Justin gazed down at the woman he loved, and the only thing he could come up with was, "Yes."

She squealed and launched herself into his arms, kissing him as passionately as she ever had. She tasted like coffee and cream, and he wanted to come home to her every night after work.

All too soon, she jumped back. She handed him the ring box. "Will you put it on?"

He gingerly removed the ring from the box, noting that the diamond had a pinkish hue to it, and the band was definitely rosy. He liked it, because it suited Renee. He locked his eyes on hers and found a storm of love in her gaze that was identical to how he felt inside.

"I love you," he said, sliding the ring on her finger.

"I love you too," she said just before kissing him again.

Five Months Later:

Renee kept smoothing her palms over her hips, though she hadn't gained any weight. She didn't even care if she'd gained weight. Didn't mind that her dress had come in at a size ten.

Every time Justin looked at her, she felt the warmth and radiating glow of his love. The past few months had been busy and then busier as she prepared for a wedding and to move into his cabin at the top of the canyon.

"Ready?" her mother asked, letting the door of the bride's room close as she turned around. "I just got the signal from your father."

Renee nodded, the vintage fifties hair rolls on her head wobbling a little. But Julia had really wanted to do her hair, and Renee wanted to include her siblings if she could. One of her brothers had provided the shoes for the wedding party. Another had purchased the flowers. Her sisters had done all the baking for the reception that evening. Renee's house looked like a flour bomb had gone off, and she couldn't wait to leave for her honeymoon—a cruise through the waters near Alaska.

Justin's brother had arrived last night, and he'd practiced the wedding with Pastor Peters and Justin while Renee entertained her gigantic family in her tiny bungalow.

Yes, everything would be better once this wedding was over.

The thought got Renee moving out the door and to her position in front of the closed chapel doors. She saw the smiling faces, but her nerves tumbled through her veins so violently, she couldn't return the gesture.

Her father took her arm, and her two brothers pulled back the doors, and her sisters started the parade into the chapel. By the time it was her turn to enter, Renee thought sure Justin would've fled.

But he hadn't.

He stood at the front of the chapel, right at the altar. Relief painted her from top to bottom. She thought sure he wouldn't show up. He'd confessed several times over the last few months that he should be the one to get to walk down the aisle while she waited for him at the altar. Then he wouldn't have to be stood up again.

No matter how many times she'd assured him she'd make it to their wedding, she'd known the worry still seethed within him.

Her father passed her to Justin, who leaned down and whispered, "You made it."

"I told you I would." She beamed up at him, and tried to infuse meaning into her next words of, "I love you."

"Ladies and gentlemen," Harvey said before Justin

could say anything in response. "We gather here today to witness the union of this man." He locked eyes with his brother. "And this woman." He looked at Renee, and she found such fire in his expression she knew he was a well-loved preacher.

"I believe they've written their own vows."

Justin fumbled a little as he released her arm and pulled his phone from his pocket. "I typed mine in a text," he said in a loud voice that filled the chapel. "See, Renee and I fell in love in sort of an unconventional way. Texts."

He met her eye and grinned. She pulled her phone out and held it up for the crowd, who twittered with laughter.

"Renee," he started. "Just because you picked me up in a bar, on a bet, doesn't mean I don't love you." He lowered his phone as she cocked her hip and glared.

"I will always love you," he said, his voice throatier and lower now. "You are my everything."

Always a man of few words, Renee thought. And actually really loved about Justin.

"My vows are much longer than that," Renee said. "Justin always let me do the talking, but I just need to say one thing. We did *not* meet in a bar."

Her family laughed the loudest, and Renee decided to wrap up this show. "Justin, I love you as much as I love ice cream."

He chuckled and they turned back to his brother, who said beautiful things about always and forever, and pronounced them husband and wife.

Renee tensed as Justin swept one hand around her waist and the other across his head to remove his cowboy hat.

"Love you, Renee," he whispered just before he kissed her to thunderous applause.

———

Keep reading for a sneak peek at the next book in the Brush Creek Cowboys series - **A Cowboy Proposal.**

Sneak Peek! A Cowboy Proposal Chapter One

Ted Caldwell whistled as he put the horse he'd worked with all morning in his stall. "You'll get it tomorrow, Yellowstone." The horse had a long way to go, but Ted just gave the animal a grin and turned toward the tack room. Yellowstone was a natural bucker, and he'd be a fantastic bronco for the rodeo if Ted could get him trained up right.

He hung up the saddle, his stomach growling for something to eat. He hadn't heard from Landon or any of the other cowboys, but Megan usually had something laid out for lunch at the homestead, especially in the summertime.

His cowboy boots made clomping noises on the packed dirt as he made his way past the exercise circle and the huge, covered horse arena. He was one of six cowboys that lived full-time at Brush Creek Horse Ranch, working and training horses for the rodeo circuit. Each of the cowboys had a different specialty, and Ted's was getting the broncos set to win championships. It could take him a couple of years to get a single horse ready, and he never worked with more than three at a time.

Right now he only had two, which gave him a bit more time to help with regular ranch duties like working in the fields and making sure the pastures stayed fenced. His spirit warmed when he thought about the weekend before him. Tomorrow afternoon, he'd take his two broncs out to the pastures by the red rock buttes, where they'd stay for a couple of days. He'd been working the horses hard lately, and everyone—himself included—needed a break.

"Landon?" he called as he entered the homestead through the sliding glass door off the pool. "Megan?" The owners of the ranch, Landon and Megan had just had their third child. Megan had only been home from the hospital for about a week, and their four-year-old twins could usually be heard from anywhere on the ranch.

But Ted couldn't hear anything right now. Neither Megan nor Landon seemed to be around, but all the sandwich stuff spread across the kitchen counter meant lunch was on at the homestead. Other cowboys had obviously been through the line, as the meat and cheese was out of the bags and the lids on the mayo and mustard had been popped.

Ted picked up his whistling again as he bustled around the kitchen, slathering mayo on white bread and then layering turkey, roast beef, and provolone on top of that. Instead of taking just a handful of chips from one of the bags, he snagged the whole, crinkly container and headed toward the front door.

The backyard baked in the Utah sun, so Megan had put

a table and enough chairs for all the cowboys to eat lunch on the front patio, where the shade kept everyone cool. As Ted exited the house, with its blessed air conditioning, he remembered how little the shade actually did in mid-July.

He sighed and took a seat at the table beside Blake, the newest member of the cowboy team at Brush Creek. "How's everyone?" He tucked a napkin into the front of his shirt and exhaled happily.

Blake chuckled. "You and that ridiculous napkin." He swiped at it, but Ted dodged him and dug into his sandwich.

"This napkin keeps my clothes pristine." He used it to wipe his beard and mustache. "And my beautiful beard lookin' great."

"For who?" Blake challenged. "Us? All the women out here are already married." He glanced across the lane to the row of cowboy cabins, two of which now housed families and not just men. Ted hadn't given much thought to expanding the residents in his cabin; he hadn't dated in the five years since he'd arrived at the ranch, since he'd left the rodeo circuit after breaking six ribs and a leg. He didn't walk with a limp, and he had enough money in the bank that he didn't have to work at all. He counted his lucky stars everyday that he'd landed at Brush Creek and could still feel the calming influence of the horses.

Walker mentioned there were lots of available women down in town, and lunch concluded. Ted stayed at the table, having only been there for a few minutes. He stretched out and put both his hands behind his head. The blue sky with those puffy white clouds made him smile.

Something crashed in the house, and Ted got to his feet,

curiosity burning through him. He wanted another sandwich anyway, so he re-entered the house, expecting to see Megan carrying her newborn and trying to keep the twins away from whatever she'd broken.

He didn't see her, but another brunette, whose hair color obviously came from a bottle, along with the numerous lighter brown and blonde streaks that fell across her shoulders.

This woman crouched low to the ground, picking up pieces of a glass bowl that had broken. She muttered under her breath and didn't seem to notice Ted as he approached —a real feat considering the size of his cowboy boots and the echoing tile floor.

"Do you need some help?" he said in his gentlest voice, the one he used on the wild horses when they first arrived at the ranch.

She jumped away from him, straightening and covering her heart with her palm. "You don't have to yell."

Ted blinked at her and looked around the house, as if someone would appear and confirm that he hadn't yelled. "I'll get the broom."

"Never mind." She looked annoyed, but surely she couldn't have a problem with him. "I'll just use a wet paper towel." Her eyes didn't land directly on his as she moved to the sink and ran the water over a half dozen paper towels. She wrung them out and then swiped the makeshift pad across the floor where the break had happened. "It gets all the tiniest pieces." She threw the paper towels in the trash and finally faced him.

Her frown deepened and she wrinkled her nose as if he smelled like horse manure. Maybe he did. "Who are you?"

"Ted Caldwell. I work with the broncos." He grinned at her, pleased when she allowed her lips to curl up slightly. "Who are you?" He allowed his eyes to travel down the length of her body, drinking in her tight jeans and billowy blouse. It was the color of shamrocks and covered with flowers.

She folded her arms. "April." Her voice indicated that he'd just used the only question she'd allow. "Excuse me." She started toward the steps that led to the basement, but her hip bumped into the sideboard and a vase teetered, tipped, toppled to the ground.

April froze as more glass, this time with real wildflowers and water, spilled across the floor. She turned back to Ted with a smile with the wattage of the sun. "Could you get the broom now?"

Ted thought he'd do whatever this woman asked, and he stepped over to the pantry like an obedient dog. He shook his head as he realized what track his thoughts had gone down. Confusion riddled through him. Ted Caldwell didn't date. Hadn't dated. Wasn't interested.

But as he turned back to April, broom in hand, he wondered if maybe it was time to *get* interested. "What's your last name, April?" he asked as he wielded the broom with precision to get all the bigger pieces of glass.

"Nox."

"Where are you from?" He threw the broken glass in the trashcan and reached for the roll of paper towels.

April leaned against the back of the couch that bordered the living room and folded her arms again. As Ted wrung out the paper towels, he noticed a distinct bump beneath her arms. His fingers stuttered and he flat-out stared.

"Wyoming," she said, her voice as sour as chokecherries. "And yes, I'm pregnant."

———

Can Ted find a way to reassure April that the hole in his life is just her size? Find out in **A Cowboy Proposal - available now in ebook, paperback, and audiobook!**

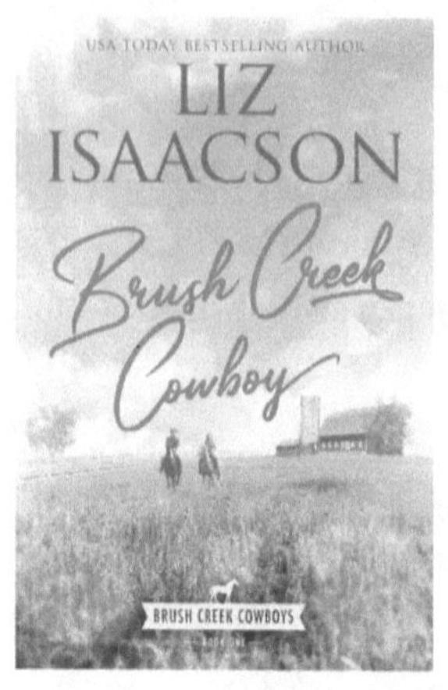

Brush Creek Cowboy (Book 1): Former rodeo champion and cowboy Walker Thompson trains horses at Brush Creek Horse Ranch, where he lives a simple life in his cabin with his ten-year-old son. A widower of six years, he's worked with Tess Wagner, a widow who came to Brush Creek to escape the turmoil of her life to give her seven-year-old son a slower pace of life. But Tess's breast cancer is back...

Walker will have to decide if he'd rather spend even a short time with Tess than not have her in his life at all. Tess wants to feel God's love and power, but can she discover and accept God's will in order to find her happy ending?

The Cowboy's Challenge (Book 2): Cowboy and professional roper Justin Jackman has found solitude at Brush Creek Horse Ranch, preferring his time with the animals he trains over dating. With two failed engagements in his past, he's not really interested in getting his heart stomped on again. But when flirty and fun Renee 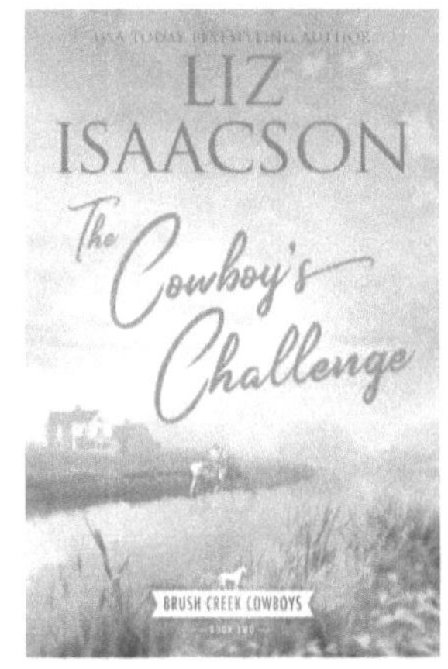Martin picks him up at a church ice cream bar--on a bet, no less--he finds himself more than just a little interested. His Gen-X attitudes are attractive to her; her Millennial behaviors drive him nuts. Can Justin look past their differences and take a chance on another engagement?

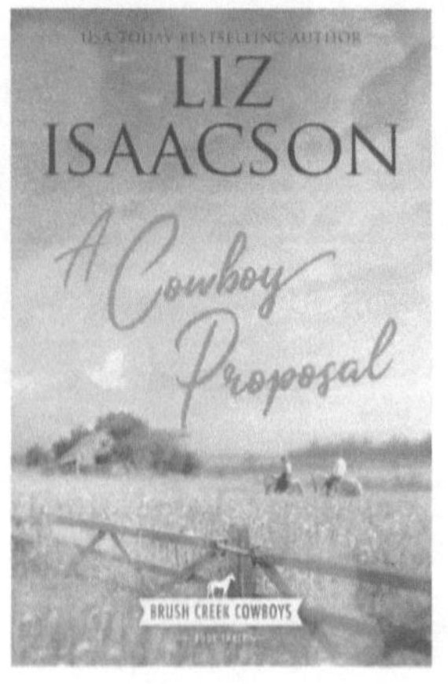

A Cowboy Proposal (Book 3): Ted Caldwell has been a retired bronc rider for years, and he thought he was perfectly happy training horses to buck at Brush Creek Ranch. He was wrong. When he meets April Nox, who comes to the ranch to hide her pregnancy from all her friends back in Jackson Hole, Ted realizes he has a huge family-shaped hole in his life. April is embarrassed, heartbroken, and trying to find her extinguished faith. She's never ridden a horse and wants nothing to do with a cowboy ever again. Can Ted and April create a family of happiness and love from a tragedy?

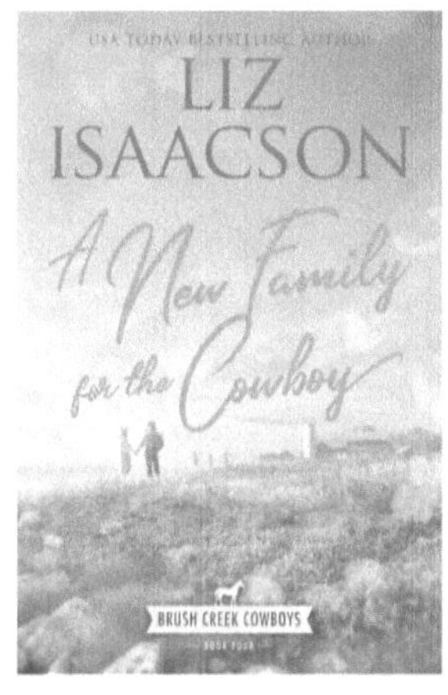

A New Family for the Cowboy (Book 4): Blake Gibbons oversees all the agriculture at Brush Creek Horse Ranch, sometimes moonlighting as a general contractor. When he meets Erin Shields, new in town, at her aunt's bakery, he's instantly smitten. Erin moved to Brush Creek after a divorce that left her penniless, homeless, and a single mother of three children under age eight. She's nowhere near ready to start dating again, but the longer Blake hangs around the bakery, the more she starts to like him. Can Blake and Erin find a way to blend their lifestyles and become a family?

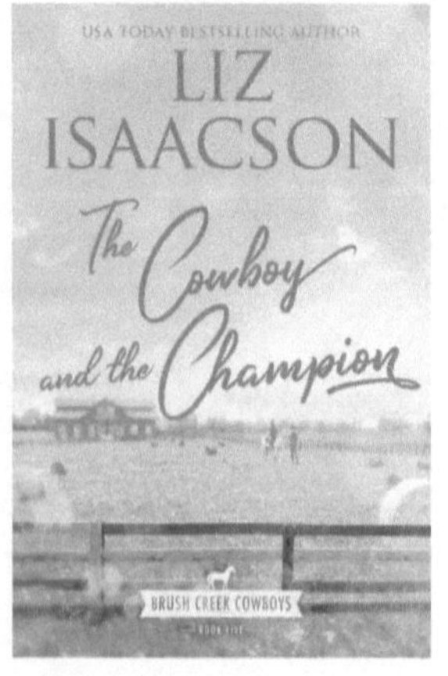 **The Cowboy and the Champion (Book 5):** Emmett Graves has always had a positive outlook on life. He adores training horses to become barrel racing champions during the day and cuddling with his cat at night. Fresh off her professional rodeo retirement, Molly Brady comes to Brush Creek Horse Ranch as Emmett's protege. He's not thrilled, and she's allergic to cats. Oh, and she'd like to stay cowboy-free, thank you very much. But Emmett's about as cowboy as they come.... Can Emmett and Molly work together without falling in love?

Schooled by the Cowboy (Book 6): Grant Ford spends his days training cattle—when he's not camped out at the elementary school hoping to catch a glimpse of his ex-girl-friend. When principal Shannon Sharpe confronts him and asks him to stay away from the school, the spark between them is instant and hot. Shan-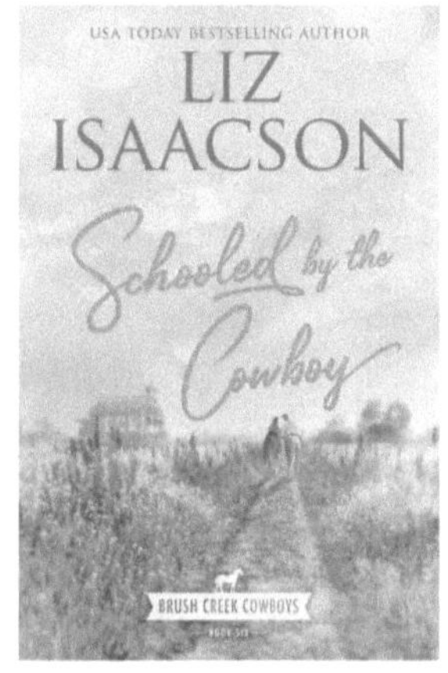
non's expecting a transfer very soon, but she also needs a summer outdoor coordinator—and Grant fits the bill. Just because he's handsome and everything Shannon's ever wanted in a cowboy husband means nothing. Will Grant and Shannon be able to survive the summer or will the Utah heat be too much for them to handle?

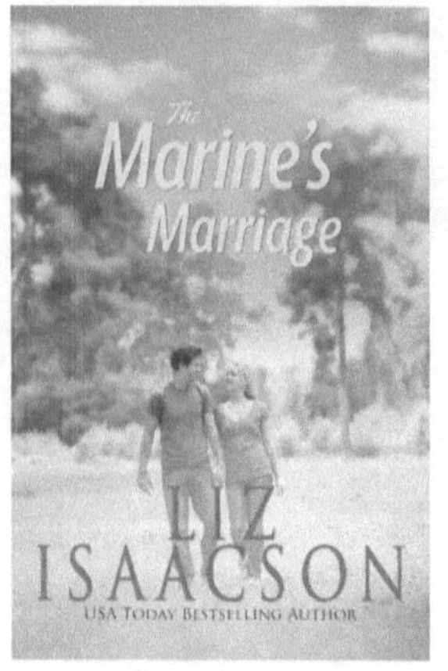

The Marine's Marriage: A Fuller Family Novel - Brush Creek Cowboys Romance (Book 1): Tate Benson can't believe he's come to Nowhere, Utah, to fix up a house that hasn't been inhabited in years. But he has. Because he's retired from the Marines and looking to start a life as a police officer in small-town Brush Creek. Wren Fuller has her hands full most days running her family's company. When Tate calls and demands a maid for that morning, she decides to have the calls forwarded to her cell and go help him out. She didn't know he was moving in next door, and she's completely unprepared for his handsomeness, his kind heart, and his wounded soul. **Can Tate and Wren weather a relationship when they're also next-door neighbors?**

The Firefighter's Fiancé: A Fuller Family Novel - Brush Creek Cowboys Romance (Book 2): Cora Wesley comes to Brush Creek, hoping to get some in-the-wild firefighting training as she prepares to put in her application to be a hotshot. When she meets Brennan Fuller, the spark between them is hot and 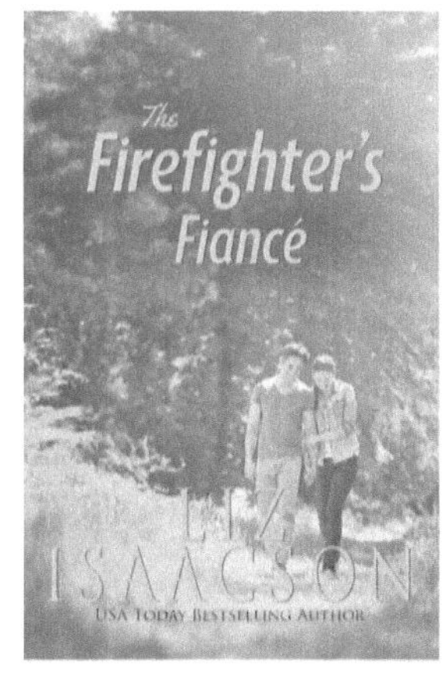 instant. As they get to know each other, her deadline is constantly looming over them, and Brennan starts to wonder if he can break ranks in the family business. He's okay mowing lawns and hanging out with his brothers, but he dreams of being able to go to college and become a landscape architect, but he's just not sure it can be done. **Will Cora and Brennan be able to endure their trials to find true love?**

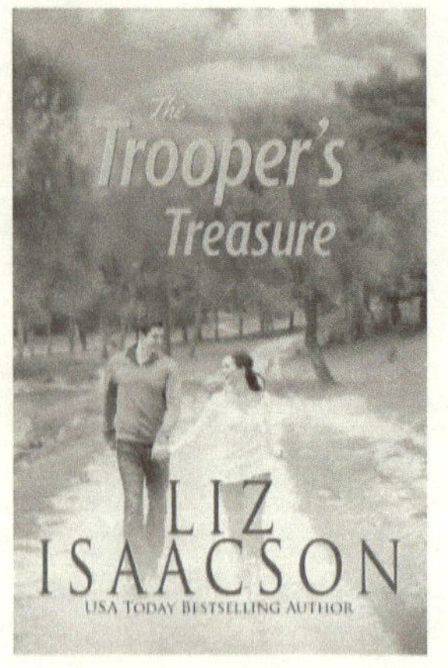

The Trooper's Treasure: A Fuller Family Novel - Brush Creek Cowboys Romance (Book 3): Dawn Fuller has made some mistakes in her life, and she's not proud of the way McDermott Boyd found her off the road one day last year. She's spent a hard year wrestling with her choices and trying to fix them, glad for McDermott's acceptance and friendship. He lost his wife years ago, done his best with his daughter, and now he's ready to move on. **Can McDermott help Dawn find a way past her former mistakes and down a path that leads to love, family, and happiness?**

The Detective's Date: A Fuller Family Novel - Brush Creek Cowboys Romance (Book 4): Dahlia Reid is one of the best detectives Brush Creek and the surrounding towns has ever had. She's given up on the idea of marriage—and pleasing her mother—and has dedicated herself fully to her job. Which is great, since one of the most

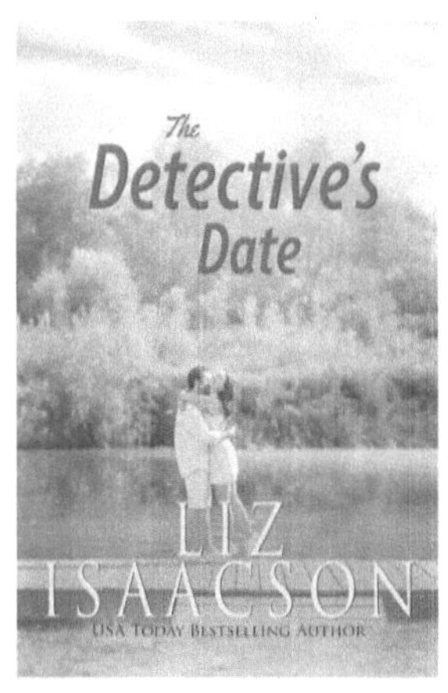

perplexing cases of her career has come to town. Kyler Fuller thinks he's finally ready to move past the woman who ghosted him years ago. He's cut his hair, and he's ready to start dating. Too bad every woman he's been out with is about as interesting as a lamppost—until Dahlia. He finds her beautiful, her quick wit a breath of fresh air, and her intelligence sexy. **Can Kyler and Dahlia use their faith to find a way through the obstacles threatening to keep them apart?**

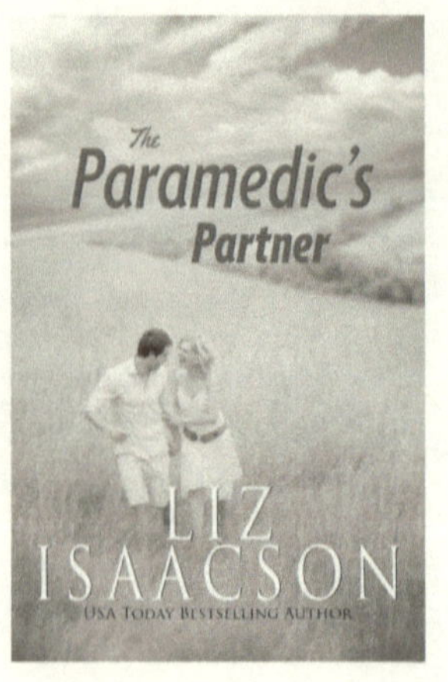

The Paramedic's Partner: A Fuller Family Novel - Brush Creek Cowboys Romance (Book 5): Jazzy Fuller has always been overshadowed by her prettier, more popular twin, Fabiana. Fabi meets paramedic Max Robinson at the park and sets a date with him only to come down with the flu. So she convinces Jazzy to cut her hair and take her place on the date. And the spark between Jazzy and Max is hot and instant...if only he knew she wasn't her sister, Fabi.

Max drives the ambulance for the town of Brush Creek with is partner Ed Moon, and neither of them have been all that lucky in love. Until Max suggests to who he thinks is Fabi that they should double with Ed and Jazzy. They do, and Fabi is smitten with the steady, strong Ed Moon. **As each twin falls further and further in love with their respective paramedic, it becomes obvious they'll need to come clean about the switcheroo sooner rather than later...or risk losing their hearts.**

The Chief's Catch: A Fuller Family Novel - Brush Creek Cowboys Romance (Book 6): Berlin Fuller has struck out with the dating scene in Brush Creek more times than she cares to admit. When she makes a deal with her friends that they can choose the next man she goes out with, she didn't dream they'd pick surly Cole Fairbanks, the new Chief of Police.

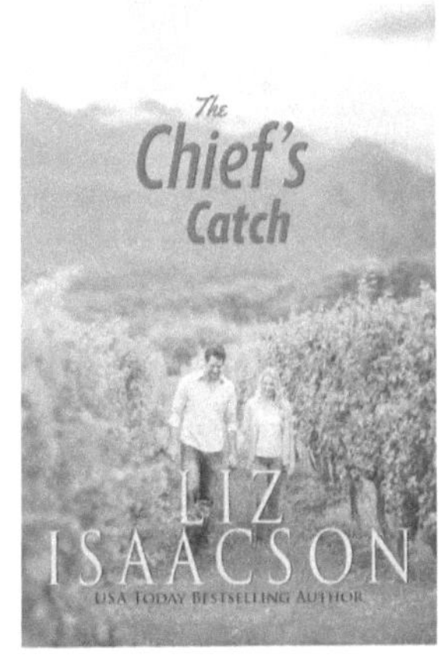

His friends call him the Beast and challenge him to complete ten dates that summer or give up his bonus check. When Berlin approaches him, stuttering about the deal with her friends and claiming they don't actually have to go out, he's intrigued. As the summer passes, Cole finds himself burning both ends of the candle to keep up with his job and his new relationship. **When he unleashes the Beast one time too many, Berlin will have to decide if she can tame him or if she should walk away.**

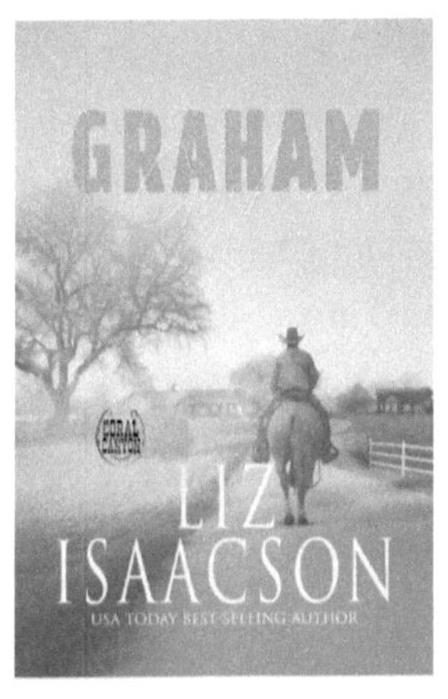

Graham (Book 1): Graham Whittaker returns to Coral Canyon a few days after Christmas—after the death of his father. He takes over the energy company his dad built from the ground up and buys a high-end lodge to live in—only a mile from the home of his once-best friend, Laney McAllister. They were best friends once, but Laney's always entertained feelings for him, and spending so much time with him while they make Christmas memories puts her heart in danger of getting broken again...

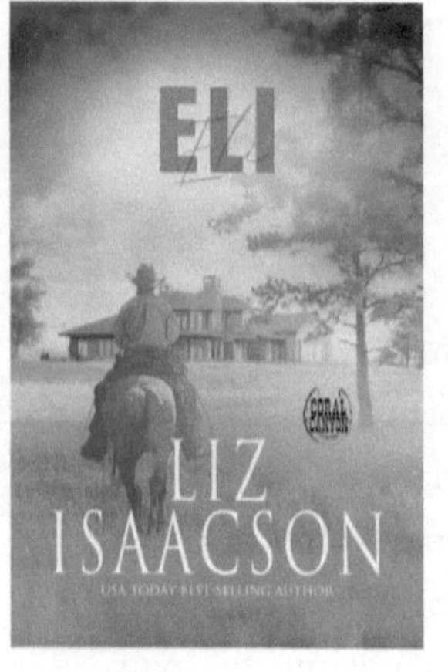

Eli (Book 2): Since the death of his wife a few years ago, Eli Whittaker has been running from one job to another, unable to find somewhere for him and his son to settle. Meg Palmer is Stockton's nanny, and she comes with her boss, Eli, to the lodge, her long-time crush on the man no different in Wyoming than it was on the beach. When she confesses her feelings for him and gets nothing in return, she's crushed, embarrassed, and unsure if she can stay in Coral Canyon for Christmas. Then Eli starts to show some feelings for her too...

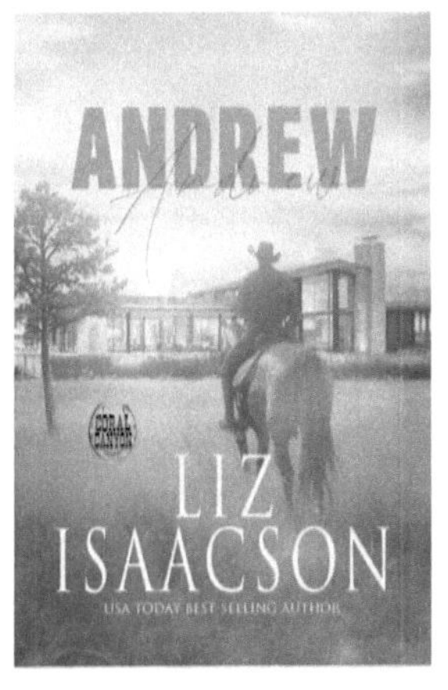

Andrew (Book 3): Andrew Whittaker is the public face for the Whittaker Brothers' family energy company, and with his older brother's robot about to be announced, he needs a press secretary to help him get everything ready and tour the state to make the announcements. When he's hit by a protest sign being carried by the company's biggest opponent, Rebecca Collings, he learns with a few clicks that she has the background they need. He offers her the job of press secretary when she thought she was going to be arrested, and not only because the spark between them in so hot Andrew can't see straight.

Can Becca and Andrew work together and keep their relationship a secret? Or will hearts break in this classic romance retelling reminiscent of *Two Weeks Notice*?

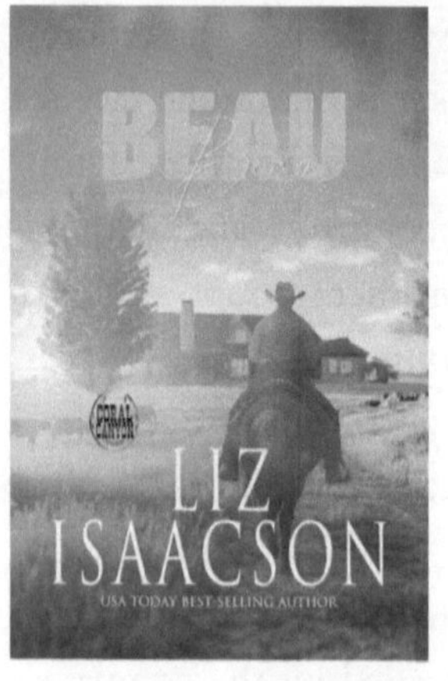

Beau (Book 4): Beau Whittaker has watched his brothers find love one by one, but every attempt he's made has ended in disaster. Lily Everett has been in the spotlight since childhood and has half a dozen platinum records with her two sisters. She's taking a break from the brutal music industry and hiding out in Wyoming while her ex-husband continues to cause trouble for her. When she hears of Beau Whittaker and what he offers his clients, she wants to meet him. Beau is instantly attracted to Lily, but he tried a relationship with his last client that left a scar that still hasn't healed...

Can Lily use the spirit of Christmas to discover what matters most? Will Beau open his heart to the possibility of love with someone so different from him?

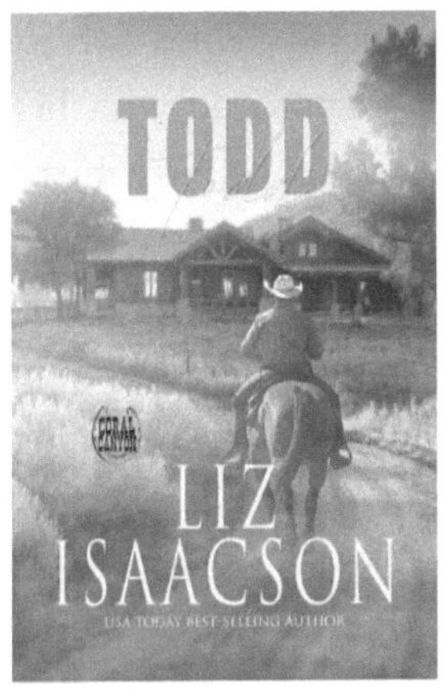

Todd (Book 5): Todd Christopherson has just retired from the professional rodeo circuit and returned to his hometown of Coral Canyon. Problem is, he's got no family there anymore, no land, and no job. Not that he needs a job--he's got plenty of money from his illustrious career riding bulls.

Then Todd gets thrown during a routine horseback ride up the canyon, and his only support as he recovers physically is the beautiful Violet Everett. She's no nurse, but she does the best she can for the handsome cowboy. **Will she lose her heart to the billionaire bull rider? Can Todd trust that God led him to Coral Canyon...and Vi?**

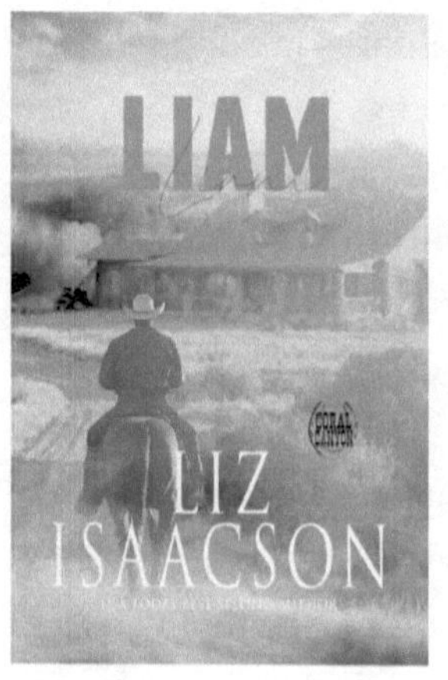

Liam (Book 6): Rose Everett isn't sure what to do with her life now that her country music career is on hold. After all, with both of her sisters in Coral Canyon, and one about to have a baby, they're not making albums anymore.

Liam Murphy has been working for Doctors Without Borders, but he's back in the US now, and looking to start a new clinic in Coral Canyon, where he spent his summers.

When Rose wins a date with Liam in a bachelor auction, their relationship blooms and grows quickly. **Can Liam and Rose find a solution to their problems that doesn't involve one of them leaving Coral Canyon with a broken heart?**

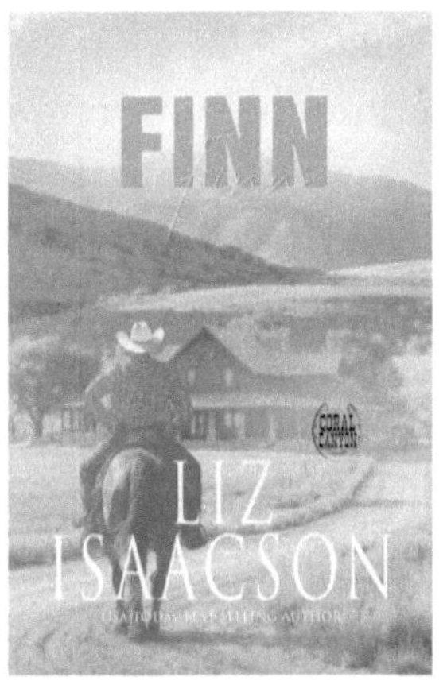

Finn (Book 7): Her sons want her to be happy, but she's too old to be set up on a blind date...isn't she?

Amanda Whittaker has been looking for a second chance at love since the death of her husband several years ago. Finley Barber is a cowboy in every sense of the word. Born and raised on a racehorse farm in Kentucky, he's since moved to Dog Valley and started his own breeding stable for champion horses. He hasn't dated in years, and everything about Amanda makes him nervous.

Will Amanda take the leap of faith required to be with Finn? Or will he become just another boyfriend who doesn't make the cut?

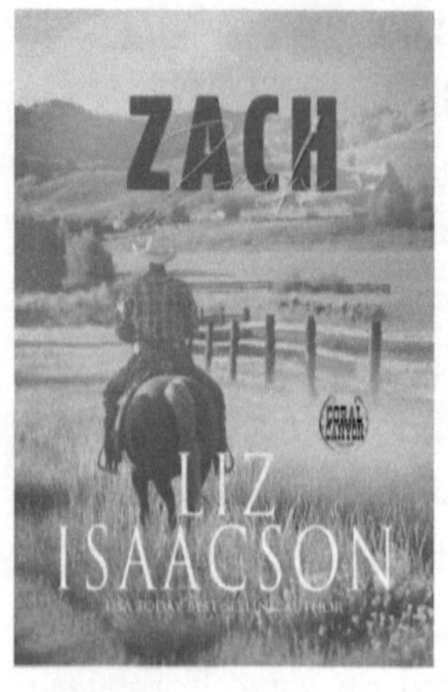

Zach (Book 8): When Celia Abbott-Armstrong runs into a gorgeous cowboy at her best friend's wedding, she decides she's ready to start dating again.

But the cowboy is Zach Zuckerman, and the Zuckermans and Abbotts have been at war for generations.

Can Zach and Celia find a way to reconcile their family's differences so they can have a future together?

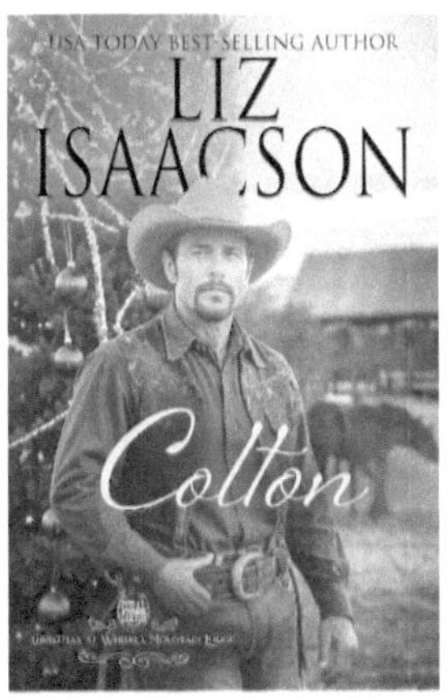

Colton (Book 1): All the maid at Whiskey Mountain Lodge wants for her birthday is a handsome cowboy billionaire. And Colton can make that wish come true—if only he hadn't escaped to Coral Canyon after being left at the altar...

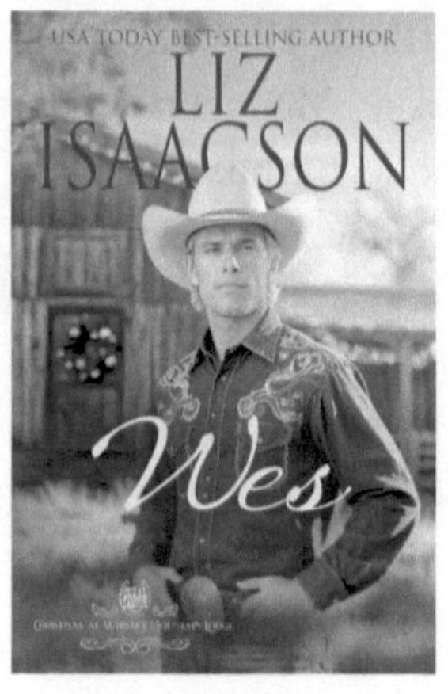

Wes (Book 2): She broke up with him to date another man...who broke her heart. He's a former CEO with nothing to do who can't get her out of his head. Can Wes and Bree find a way toward happily-ever-after at Whiskey Mountain Lodge?

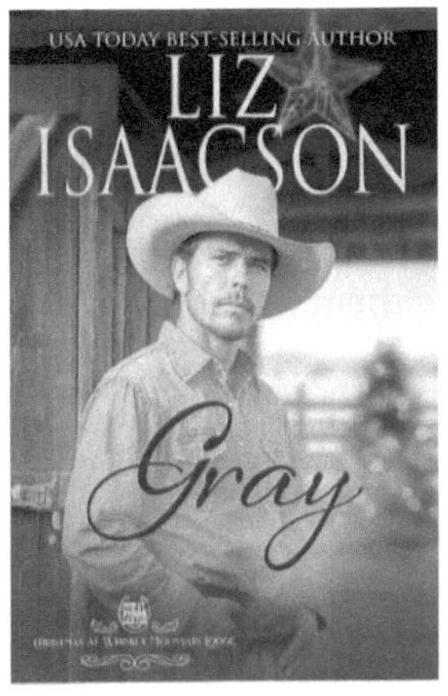

Gray (Book 3): She's best friends with the single dad cowboy's brother and has watched two friends find love with the sexy new cowboys in town. When Gray Hammond comes to Whiskey Mountain Lodge with his son, will Elise finally get her own happily-ever-after with one of the Hammond brothers?

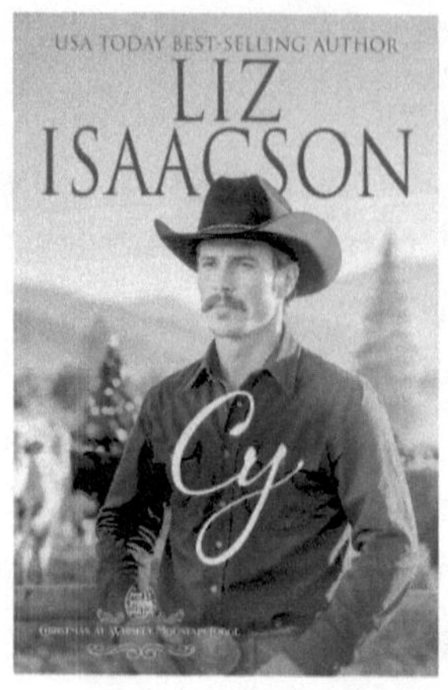

Cy (Book 4): A cowboy billionaire beast, his new manager, and the Christmas traditions that soften his heart and bring them together.

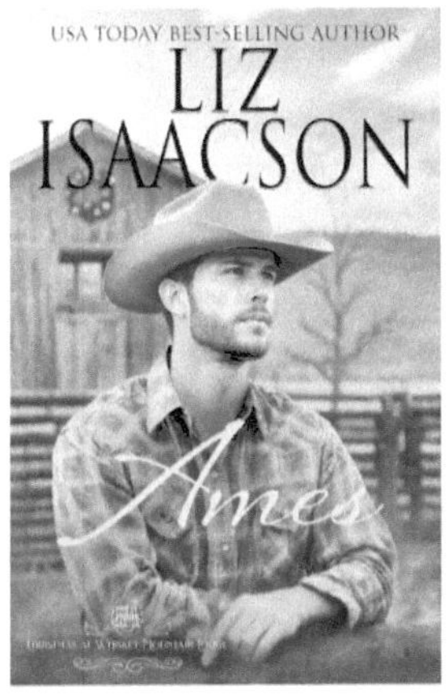

Ames (Book 5): A cowboy billionaire cop who's a stickler for rules, the woman he pulls over when he's not even on duty, and the personal mandates he has to break to keep her in his life...

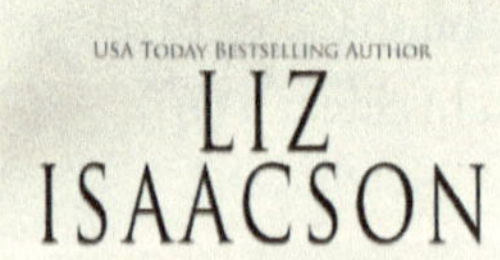

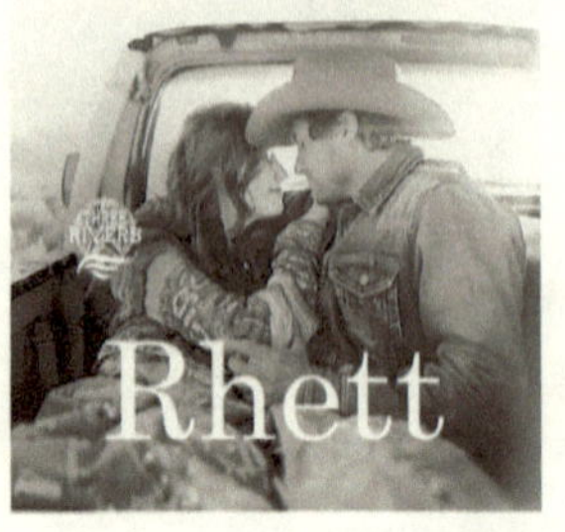

Rhett (Book 1): To save her business, she'll have to risk her heart. She needs a husband to be credible as a matchmaker. He wants to help a neighbor. **Will their fake marriage take them out of the friend zone?**

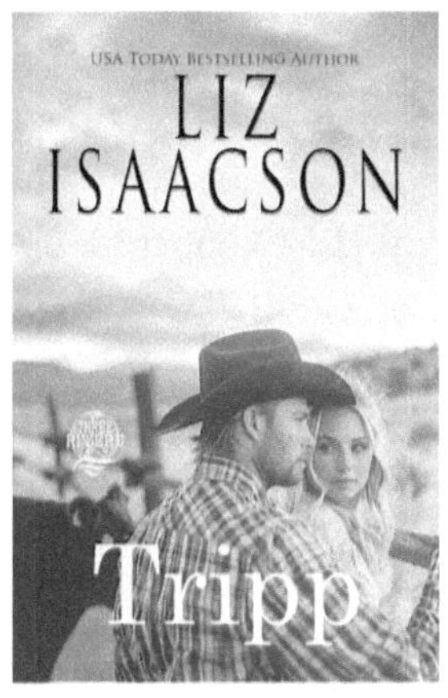

Tripp (Book 2): She needs a husband to keep her son. He's wanted to take their relationship to the next level, but she's always pushing him away. Will their trivial tie take them all the way to happily-ever-after?

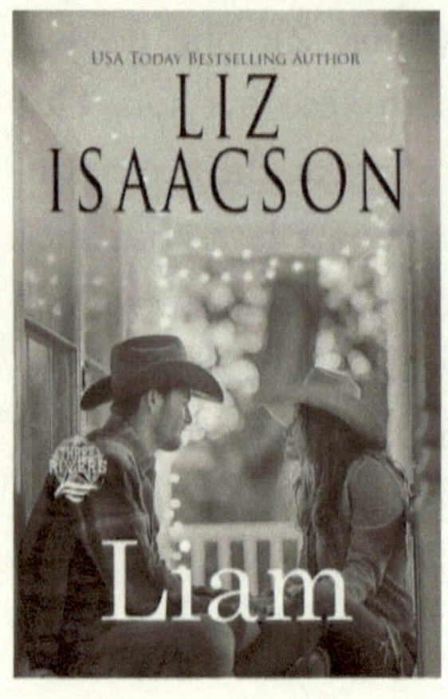

Liam (Book 3): She's desperate to save her ranch. He wants to help her any way he can. Will their invented I-Do open doors that have previously been closed and lead to a happily-ever-after for both of them?

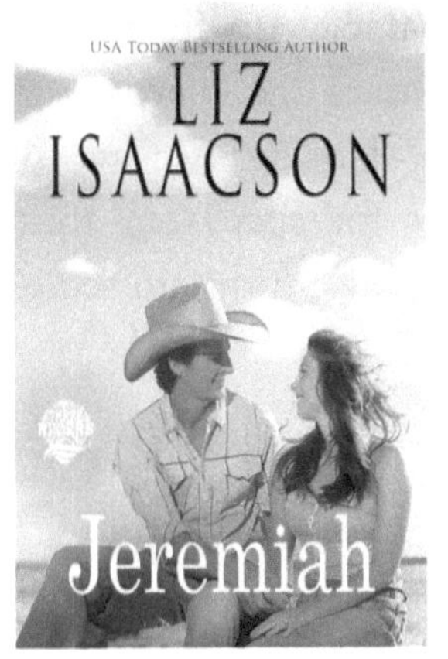

Jeremiah (Book 4): He wants to prove to his brothers that he's not broken. She just wants him. Will a fake marriage heal him or push her further away?

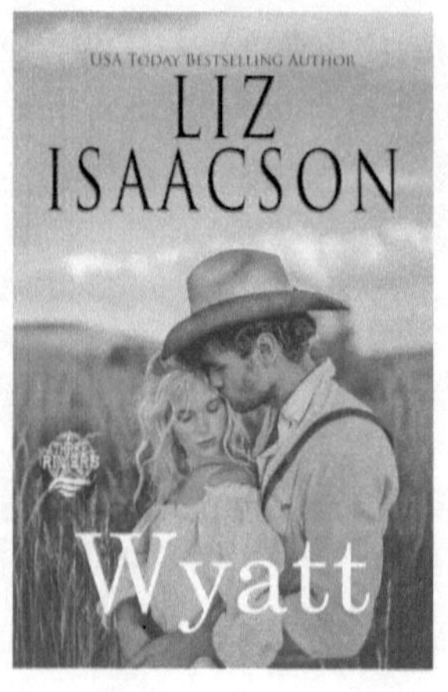

Wyatt (Book 5): To get her inheritance, she needs a husband. He's wanted to fly with her for ages. Can their pretend pledge turn into something real?

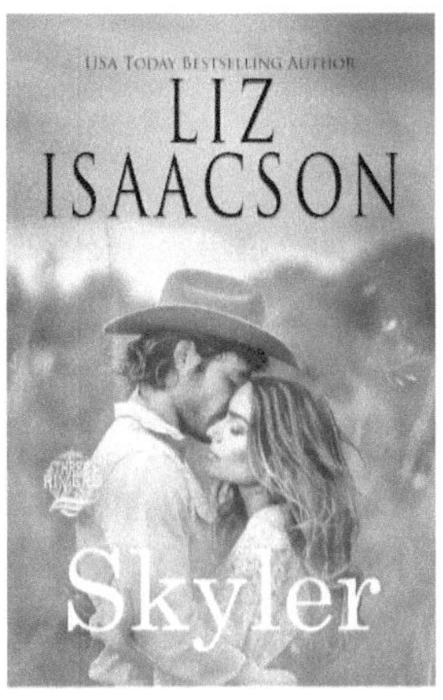

Skyler (Book 6): She needs a new last name to stay in school. He's willing to help a fellow student. Can this wanna-be wife show the playboy that some things should be taken seriously?

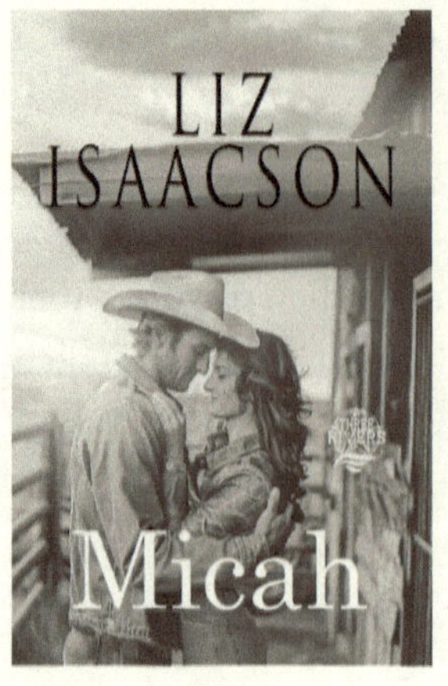

Micah (Book 7): They were just actors auditioning for a play. The marriage was just for the audition – until a clerical error results in a legal marriage. Can these two ex-lovers negotiate this new ground between them and achieve new roles in each other's lives?

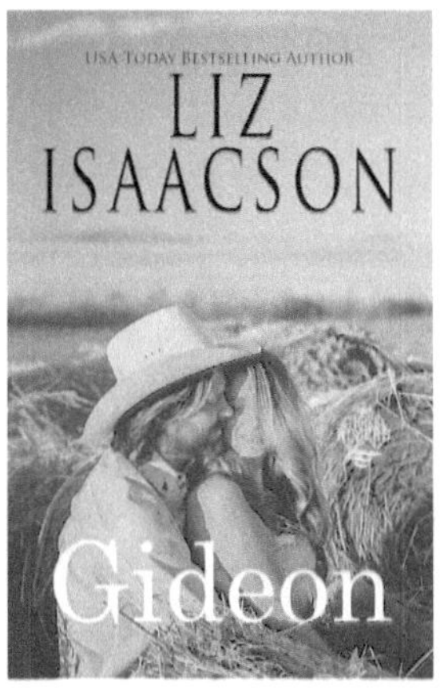

Gideon (Book 8): It's 1971, and Gideon Walker is on the cutting edge of all the technology coming out of Texas. He has big dreams and wants to make something of himself. Then he meets Penny Aarons, and everything changes. He only has eyes for her, but she's got plans and dreams of her own...

Read this origin romance for Momma and Daddy from the Seven Sons series today!

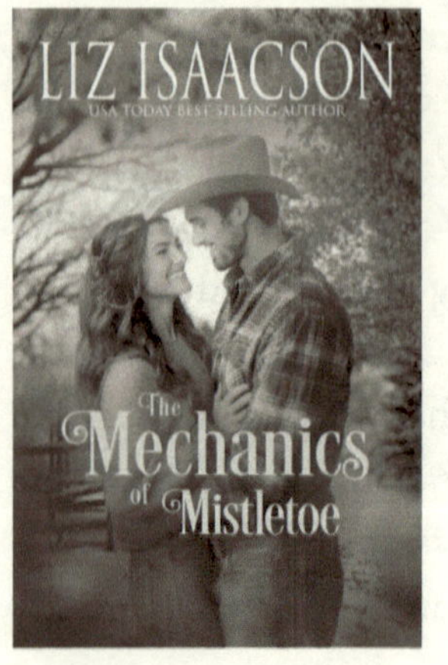

The Mechanics of Mistletoe (Book 1): Bear Glover can be a grizzly or a teddy, and he's always thought he'd be just fine working his generational family ranch and going back to the ancient homestead alone. But his crush on Samantha Benton won't go away. She's a genius with a wrench on Bear's tractors...and his heart. Can he tame his wild side and get the girl, or will he be left brokenhearted this Christmas season?

The Horsepower of the Holiday (Book 2): Ranger Glover has worked at Shiloh Ridge Ranch his entire life. The cowboys do everything from horseback there, but when he goes to town to trade in some trucks, somehow Oakley Hatch persuades him to take some ATVs back to the ranch. (Bear is NOT happy.)

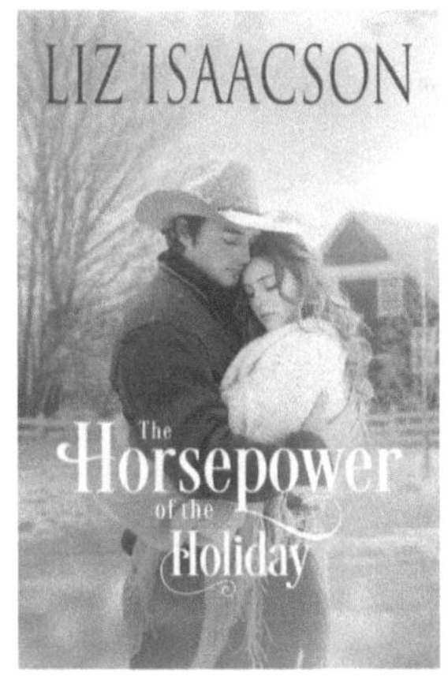

She's a former race car driver who's got Ranger all revved up... Can he remember who he is and get Oakley to slow down enough to fall in love, or will there simply be too much horsepower in the holiday this year for a real relationship?

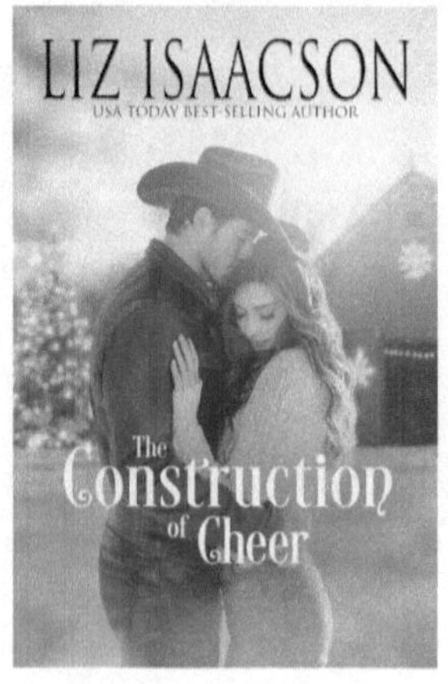

The Construction of Cheer (Book 3): Bishop Glover is the youngest brother, and he usually keeps his head down and gets the job done. When Montana Martin shows up at Shiloh Ridge Ranch looking for work, he finds himself inventing construction projects that need doing just to keep her coming around. (Again, Bear is NOT happy.) She wants to build her own construction firm, but she ends up carving a place for herself inside Bishop's heart. Can he convince her *he's* all she needs this Christmas season, or will her cheer rest solely on the success of her business?

The Secret of Santa (Book 4):
He's a fun-loving cowboy with a heart of gold. She's the woman who keeps putting him on hold. Can Ace and Holly Ann make a relationship work this Christmas?

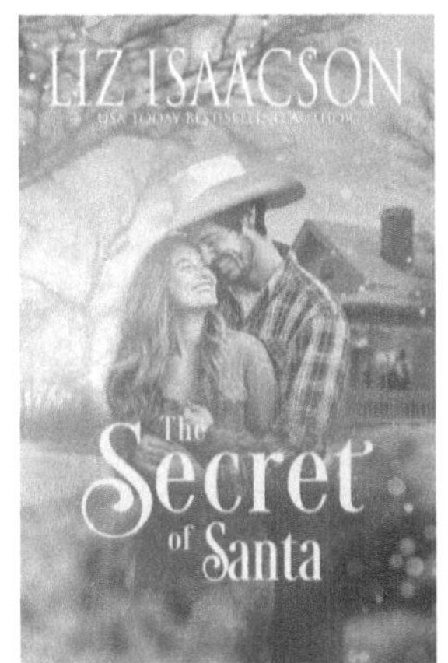

The Gift of Gingerbread (Book 5): She's the only daughter in the Glover family. He's got a secret that drove him out of town years ago. Can Arizona and Duke find common ground and their happily-ever-after this Christmas?

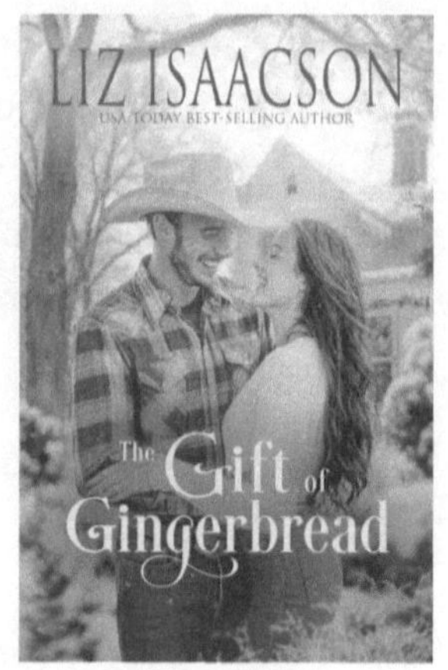

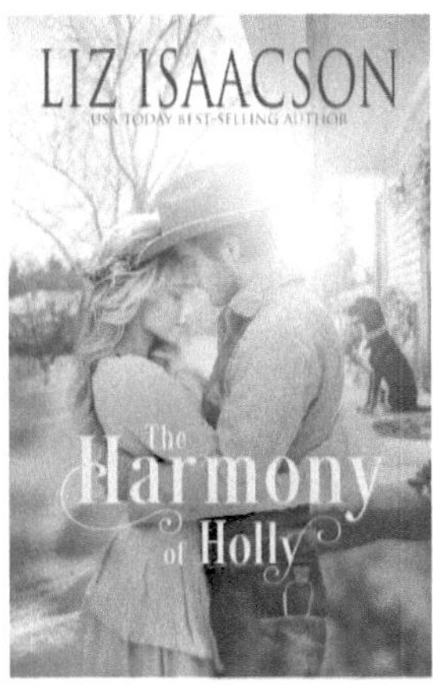

The Harmony of Holly (Book 6): He's as prickly as his name, but the new woman in town has caught his eye. Can Cactus shelve his temper and shed his cowboy hermit skin fast enough to make a relationship with Willa work?

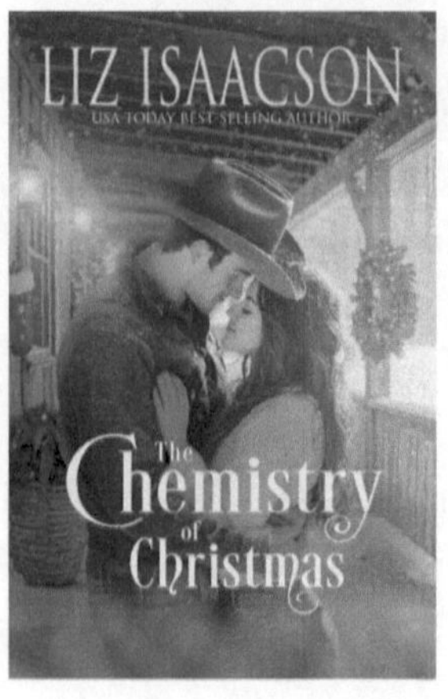

The Chemistry of Christmas (Book 7): He's the black sheep of the family, and she's a chemist who understands formulas, not emotions. Can Preacher and Charlie take their quirks and turn them into a strong relationship this Christmas?

The Delivery of Decor (Book 8): When he falls, he falls hard and deep. She literally drives away from every relationship she's ever had. Can Ward somehow get Dot to stay this Christmas?

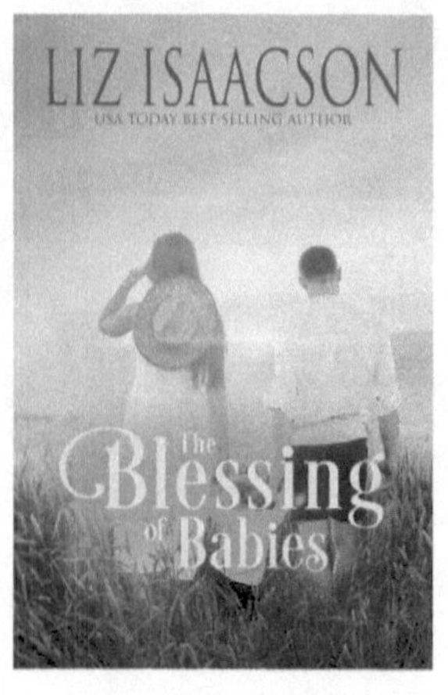

The Blessing of Babies (Book 9): Don't miss out on a single moment of the Glover family saga in this bridge story linking Ward and Judge's love stories!

The Glovers love God, country, dogs, horses, and family. Not necessarily in that order. ;)

Many of them are married now, with babies on the way, and there are lessons to be learned, forgiveness to be had and given, and new names coming to the family tree in southern Three Rivers!

The Networking of the Nativity (Book 10): He's had a crush on her for years. She doesn't want to date until her daughter is out of the house. Will June take a change on Judge when the success of his Christmas light display depends on her networking abilities?

The Yes at Yuletide (Book 11): If they can't find a way to bridge the gap between their aspirations and their love, this winter wedding could be the last holiday they spend side by side. Will Ollie and Aurora discover a path that keeps their hearts—and their dreams—together, or will this Christmas be the beginning of a new kind of goodbye?

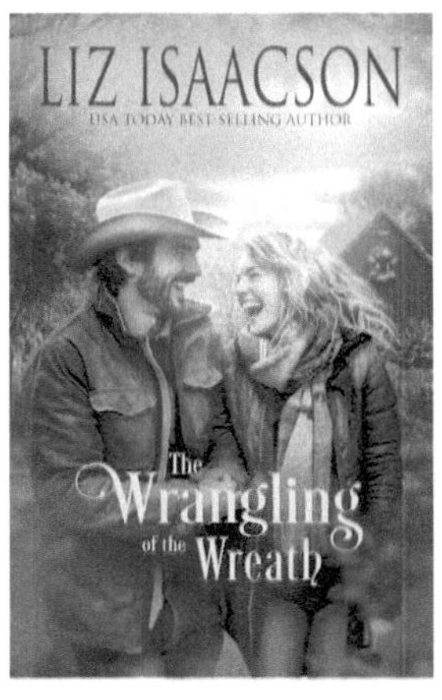

The Wrangling of the Wreath (Book 12): He's been so busy trying to find Miss Right. She's been right in front of him the whole time. This Christmas, can Mister and Libby take their relationship out of the best friend zone?

The Hope of Her Heart (Book 13): She's the only Glover without a significant other. He's been searching for someone who can love him *and* his daughter. Can Etta and August make a meaningful connection this Christmas?

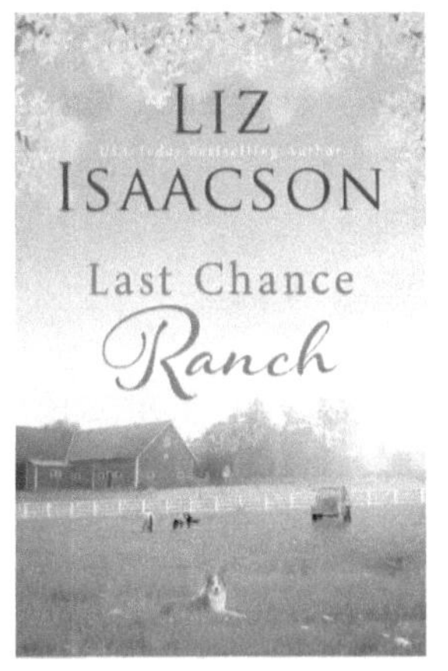

Last Chance Ranch (Book 1): A cowgirl down on her luck hires a man who's good with horses and under the hood of a car. Can Hudson fine tune Scarlett's heart as they work together? Or will things backfire and make everything worse at Last Chance Ranch?

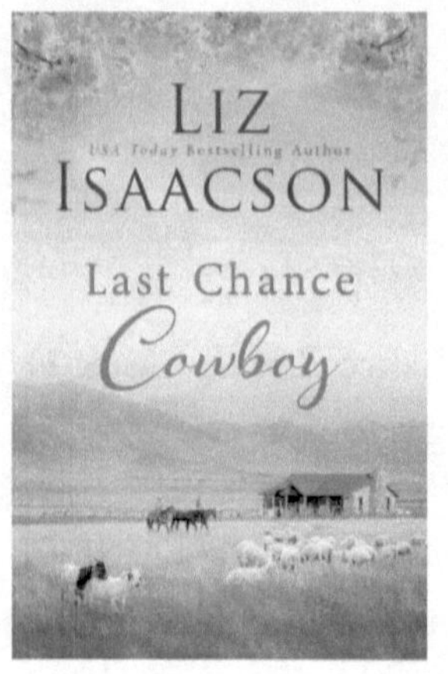

Last Chance Cowboy (Book 2): A billionaire cowboy without a home meets a woman who secretly makes food videos to pay her debts...Can Carson and Adele do more than fight in the kitchens at Last Chance Ranch?

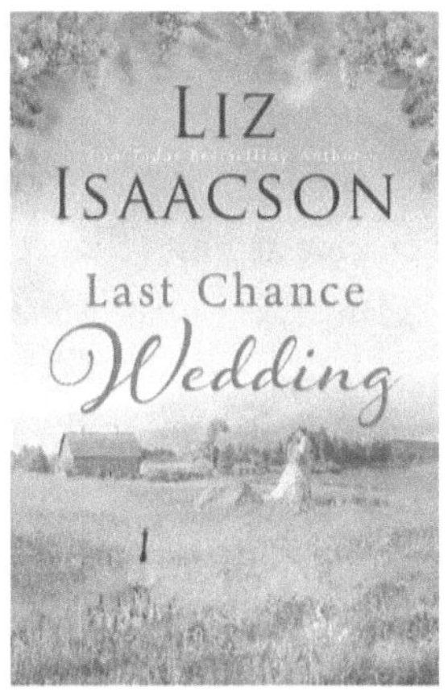

Last Chance Wedding (Book 3): A female carpenter needs a husband just for a few days... Can Jeri and Sawyer navigate the minefield of a pretend marriage before their feelings become real?

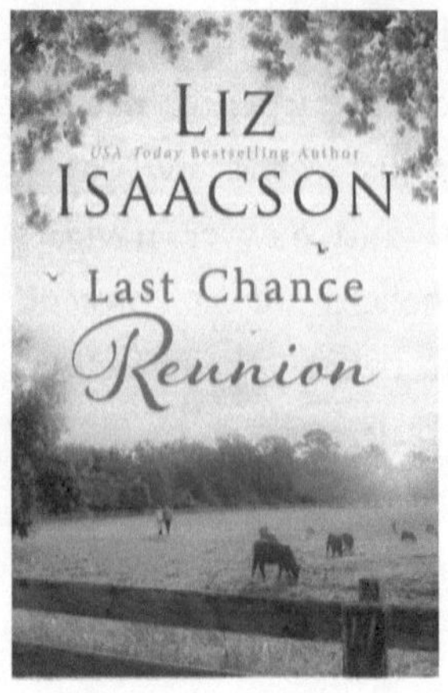

Last Chance Reunion (Book 4): An Army cowboy, the woman he dated years ago, and their last chance at Last Chance Ranch... Can Dave and Sissy put aside hurt feelings and make their second chance romance work?

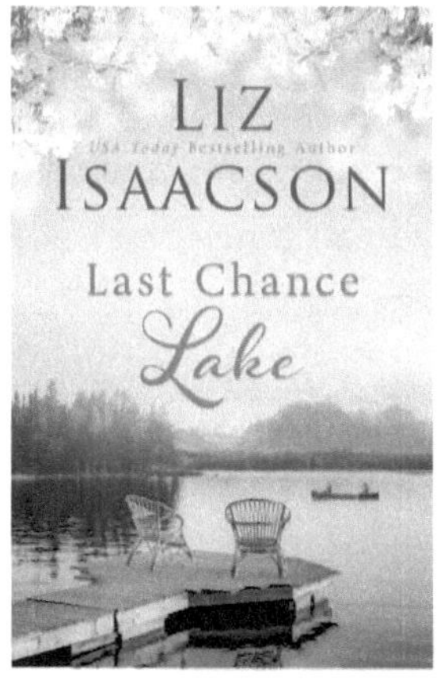 **Last Chance Lake (Book 5):** A former dairy farmer and the marketing director on the ranch have to work together to make the cow cuddling program a success. But can Karla let Cache into her life? Or will she keep all her secrets from him - and keep *him* a secret too?

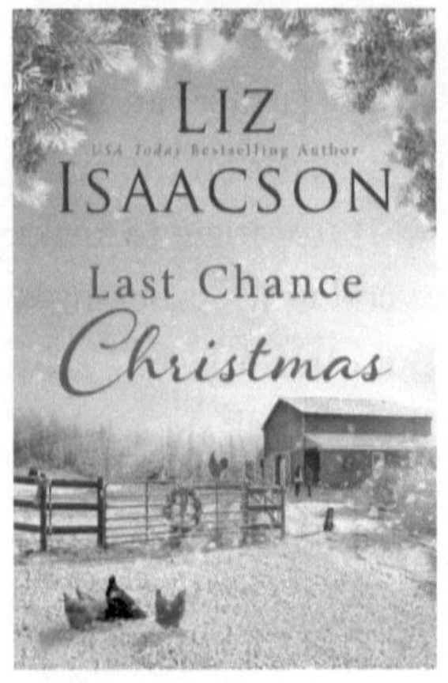

Last Chance Christmas (Book 6): She's tired of having her heart broken by cowboys. He waited too long to ask her out. Can Lance fix things quickly, or will Amber leave Last Chance Ranch before he can tell her how he feels?

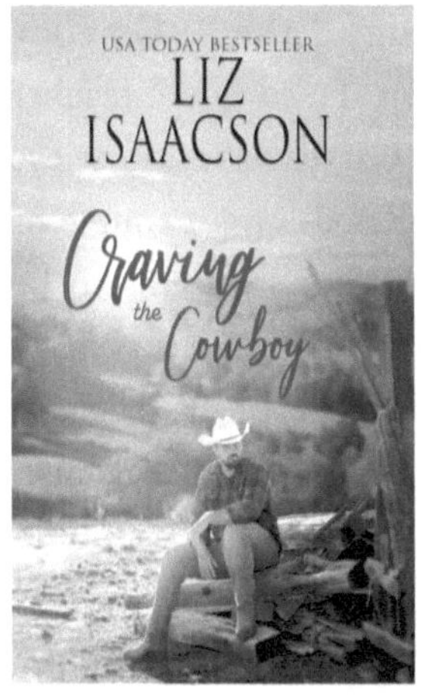

Craving the Cowboy (Book 1): Dwayne Carver is set to inherit his family's ranch in the heart of Texas Hill Country, and in order to keep up with his ranch duties and fulfill his dreams of owning a horse farm, he hires top trainer Felicity Lightburne. They get along great, and she can envision herself on this new farm—at least until her mother falls ill and she has to return to help her. Can Dwayne and Felicity work through their differences to find their happily-ever-after?

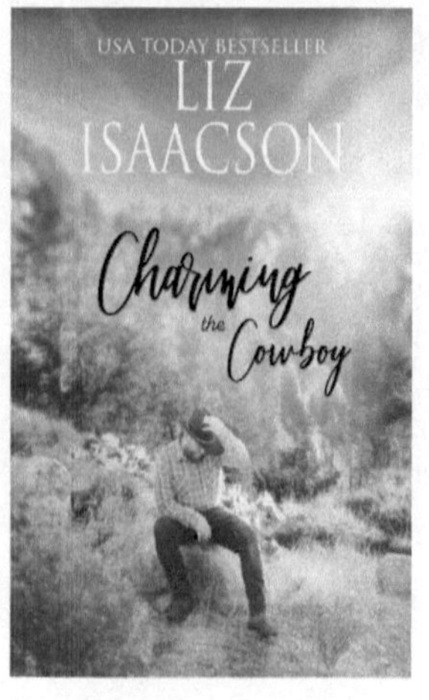

Charming the Cowboy (Book 2): Third grade teacher Heather Carver has had her eye on Levi Rhodes for a couple of years now, but he seems to be blind to her attempts to charm him. When she breaks her arm while on his horse ranch, Heather infiltrates Levi's life in ways he's never thought of, and his strict anti-female stance slips. Will Heather heal his emotional scars and he care for her physical ones so they can have a real relationship?

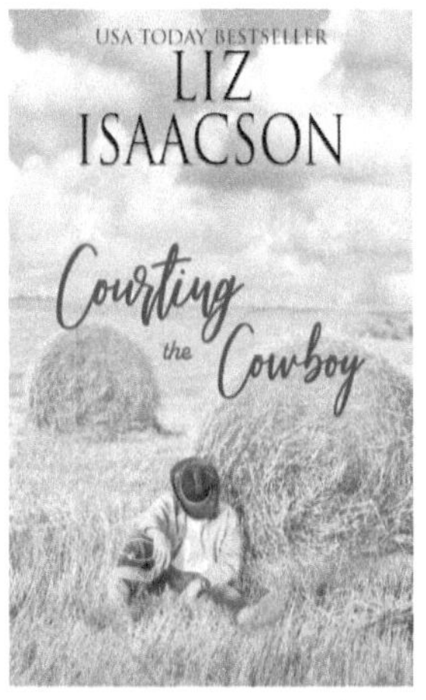

Courting the Cowboy (Book 3): Frustrated with the cowboy-only dating scene in Grape Seed Falls, May Sotheby joins Texas-Faithful.com, hoping to find her soul mate without having to relocate--or deal with cowboy hats and boots. She has no idea that Kurt Pemberton, foreman at Grape Seed Ranch, is the man she starts communicating with... Will May be able to follow her heart and get Kurt to forgive her so they can be together?

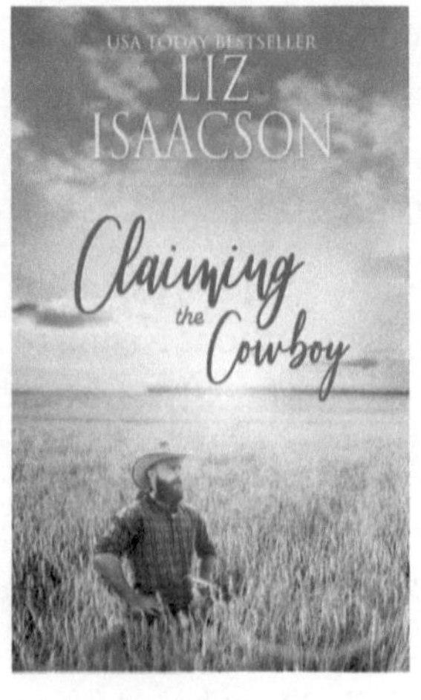

Claiming the Cowboy, Royal Brothers Book 1 (Grape Seed Falls Romance Book 4): Unwilling to be tied down, farrier Robin Cook has managed to pack her entire life into a two-hundred-and-eighty square-foot house, and that includes her Yorkie. Cowboy and co-foreman, Shane Royal has had his heart set on Robin for three years, even though she flat-out turned him down the last time he asked her to dinner. But she's back at Grape Seed Ranch for five weeks as she works her horseshoeing magic, and he's still interested, despite a bitter life lesson that left a bad taste for marriage in his mouth.

Robin's interested in him too. But can she find room for Shane in her tiny house--and can he take a chance on her with his tired heart?

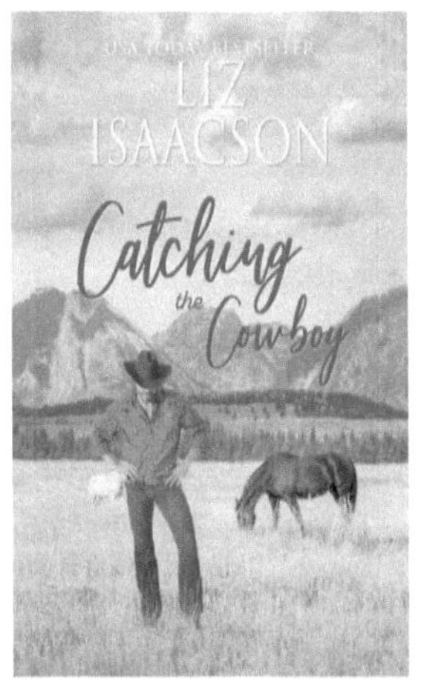

Catching the Cowboy, Royal Brothers Book 2 (Grape Seed Falls Romance Book 5): Dylan Royal is good at two things: whistling and caring for cattle. When his cows are being attacked by an unknown wild animal, he calls Texas Parks & Wildlife for help. He wasn't expecting a beautiful mammologist to show up, all flirty and fun and everything Dylan didn't know he wanted in his life.

Hazel Brewster has gone on more first dates than anyone in Grape Seed Falls, and she thinks maybe Dylan deserves a second... Can they find their way through wild animals, huge life changes, and their emotional pasts to find their forever future?

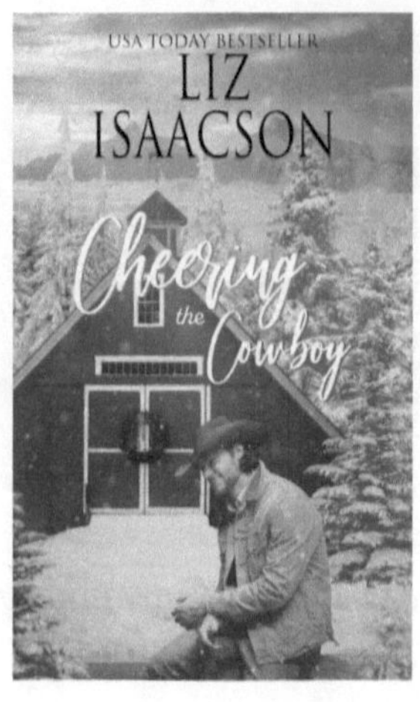

Cheering the Cowboy, Royal Brothers Book 3 (Grape Seed Falls Romance Book 6): Austin Royal loves his life on his new ranch with his brothers. But he doesn't love that Shayleigh Hatch came with the property, nor that he has to take the blame for the fact that he now owns her childhood ranch. They rarely have a conversation that doesn't leave him furious and frustrated--and yet he's still attracted to Shay in a strange, new way.

Shay inexplicably likes him too, which utterly confuses and angers her. As they work to make this Christmas the best the Triple Towers Ranch has ever seen, can they also navigate through their rocky relationship to smoother waters?

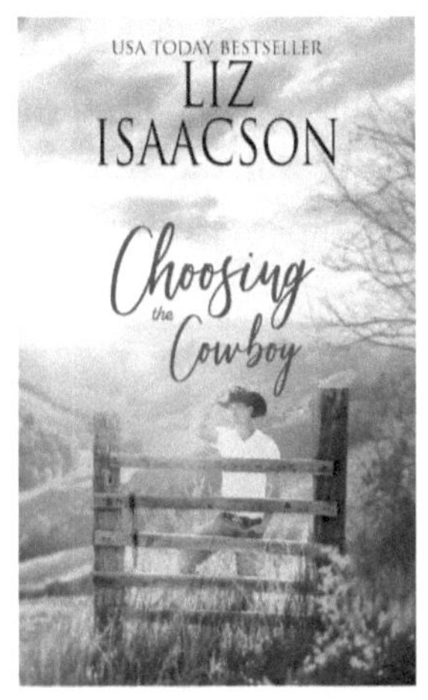

Choosing the Cowboy (Book 7): With financial trouble and personal issues around every corner, can Maggie Duffin and Chase Carver rely on their faith to find their happily-ever-after?

A spinoff from the #1 bestselling Three Rivers Ranch Romance novels, also by USA Today bestselling author Liz Isaacson.

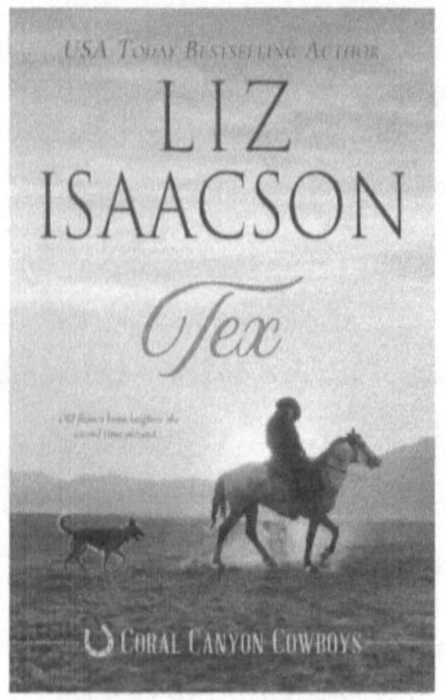

Tex (Book 1): He's back in town after a successful country music career. She owns a bordering farm to the family land he wants to buy...and she outbids him at the auction. Can Tex and Abigail rekindle their old flame, or will the issue of land ownership come between them?

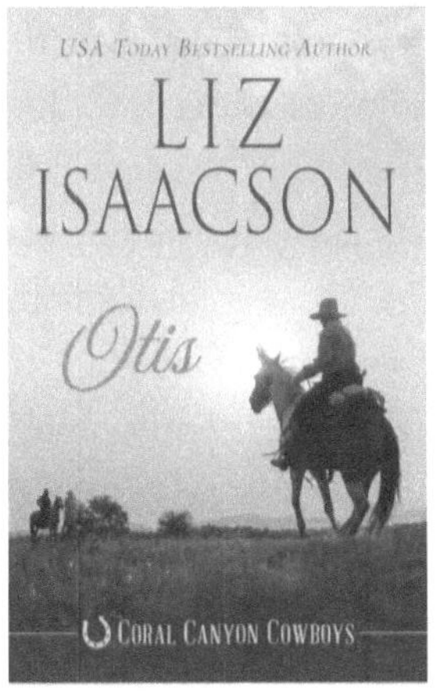

Otis (Book 2): He's finished with his last album and looking for a soft place to fall after a devastating break-up. She runs the small town bookshop in Coral Canyon and needs a new boyfriend to get her old one out of her life for good. Can Georgia convince Otis to take another shot at real love when their first kiss was fake?

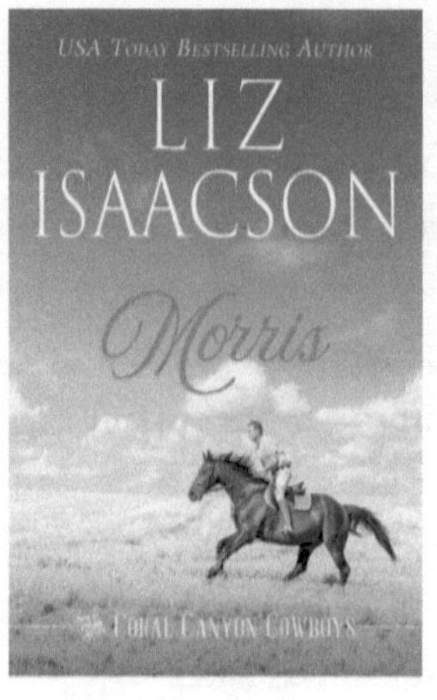

Morris (Book 3): Morris Young is just settling into his new life as the manager of Country Quad when he attends a wedding. He sees his ex-wife there—apparently Leighann is back in Coral Canyon—along with a little boy who can't be more or less than five years old... Could he be Morris's? And why is his heart hoping for that, and for a reconciliation with the woman who left him because he traveled too much?

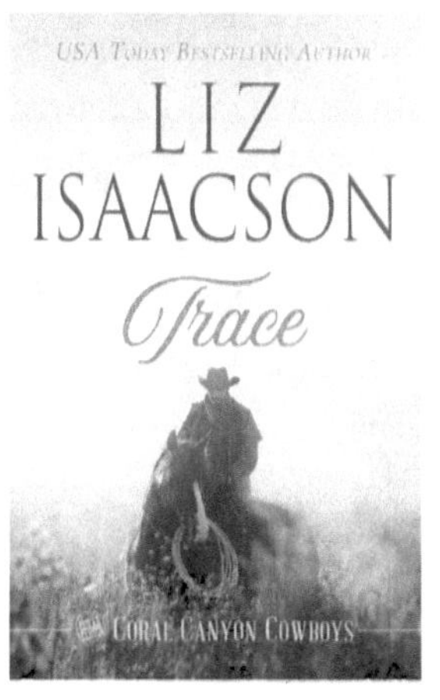

Trace (Book 4): He's been accused of only dating celebrities. She's a simple line dance instructor in small town Coral Canyon, with a soft spot for kids...and cowboys. Trace could use some dance lessons to go along with his love lessons... Can he and Everly fall in love with the beat, or will she dance her way right out of his arms?

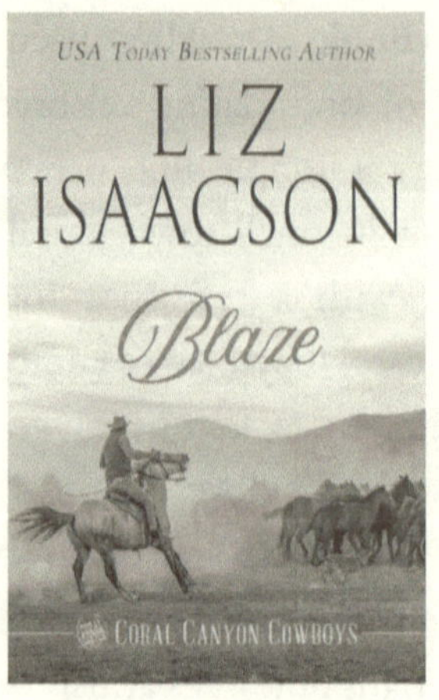

Blaze (Book 5): He's dark as night, a single dad, and a retired bull riding champion. With all his money, his rugged good looks, and his ability to say all the right things, Faith has no chance against Blaze Young's charms. But she's his complete opposite, and she just doesn't see how they can be together...

...so she ends things with him.

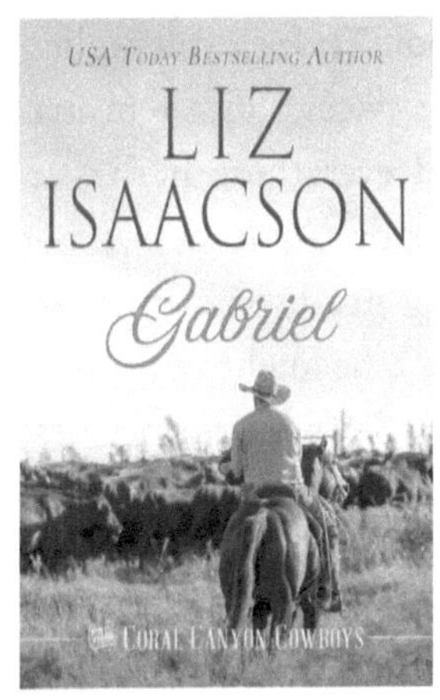

Gabe (Book 6): He's a father's rights advocate lawyer with a sweet little girl. She's fighting for her own daughter. Can Gabe and Hilde find happily-ever-after when they're at such odds with one another?

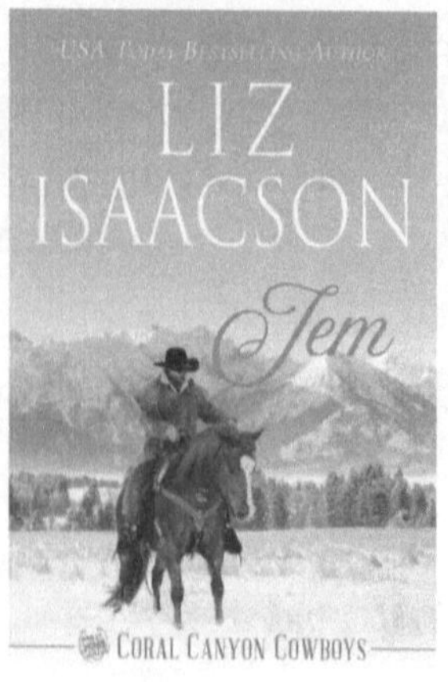

Jem (Book 7): He's still healing from his vices, and Jem has dedicated everything he has to his two kids. At least he's not mourning his divorce anymore, and in fact, he might be ready to move on. She's his former best friend, and once he breaks his wrist, his nurse. Can Sunny somehow rope this cowboy's heart?

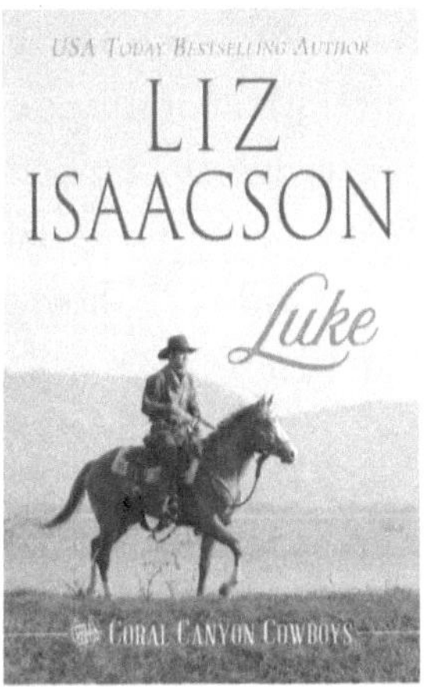

Luke (Book 8): He swore off women when his ex told him he might not be their daughter's father. But a paternity test confirmed he is, and Luke Young has dedicated his life to his little girl and his brothers' band. There hasn't been time for a girlfriend anyway. He's tried here and there, and the women in small-town Coral Canyon are certainly interested in him.

But he's been thinking about his massage therapist for a while now. Can he ask Sterling out when all they've ever been is professional? Oh, and there's the fact that she's seen practically every inch of his body... Awkward, right?

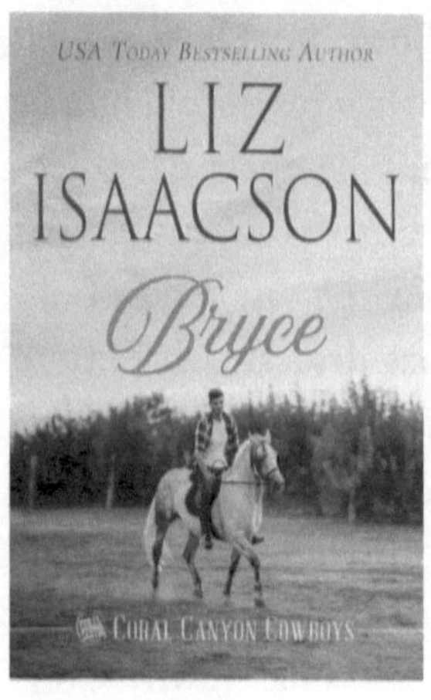

Bryce (Book 9): Bryce Young has been broken and drifting for years. After giving up his son for adoption, he left Coral Canyon and hasn't returned...until now.

ABOUT LIZ

Liz Isaacson writes inspirational romance, usually set in Texas, or Wyoming, or anywhere else horses and cowboys exist. She lives in Utah, where she writes full-time, takes her two dogs to the park everyday, and eats a lot of veggies while writing. Find her on her website at feelgoodfiction-books.com